POWER ⚡

THE OFFICIAL MOVIE NOVEL

ADAPTED BY
ALEX IRVINE

BASED ON THE
SCREENPLAY BY
JOHN GATINS

BASED UPON
"POWER RANGERS"
CREATED BY
HAIM SABAN AND
TOEI COMPANY LTD.

PENGUIN YOUNG READERS LICENSES
AN IMPRINT OF PENGUIN RANDOM HOUSE

PENGUIN YOUNG READERS LICENSES
An Imprint of Penguin Random House LLC

Cover design by Gabriel P. Cooper

ISBN 9780515159691   10 9 8 7 6 5 4 3 2 1

SABAN'S

POWER RANGERS
THE OFFICIAL MOVIE NOVEL

SPECIAL THANKS TO
HAIM SABAN
AND
THE REST OF THE FILMMAKERS
AS WELL AS
EVERYONE AT SABAN BRANDS,
LIONSGATE,
AND
TEMPLE HILL ENTERTAINMENT

PROLOGUE

The Red Ranger knew he was going to die. Here on this distant planet, surrounded by the huge native creatures. Some of them, long-necked and curious, watched from the shallows of the nearby ocean. He dragged himself through the dirt, mud, and torn-up landscape. Behind him a spaceship crashed, catapulting him over the broken earth. Intent on his mission—his last mission—he kept crawling. Debris and crushed rock cascaded down around him. He got to the Yellow Ranger, and her armor peeled away. She knew what was going to happen just like the Red Ranger did.

"I'm sorry," he said, taking her coin. He already had three others: black, blue, pink. Her eyes closed. She was gone.

He sent a message on the emergency frequency. "I'm the last one left. Commence destruction." He had no choice. In less than a minute it would all be over.

The Red Ranger pulled a small tree root from the destroyed soil. When he had dug a pit deep enough for them to be safe, he placed the coins in the muddy bottom. Finally, he removed his own coin, demorphing in the process.

Placing the coin alongside the others, the Red Ranger whispered, "Seek only those who are worthy. Find only those who are strong."

A boot crunched on the gravel near him. The Red Ranger looked up, unable to stand. Towering over him was the Green Ranger, Rita Repulsa, her golden staff planted in the ground. Once, the two had fought together. Then they had become enemies when Rita betrayed the Power Rangers' mission.

"It's time to tell me where the Zeo Crystal is," she hissed.

"That was never going to happen," the Red Ranger said.

She nodded at him. "Then you will die with all your friends, Zordon."

She raised her golden staff for a killing blow—but paused as a rumbling sound filled the air.

A massive asteroid burned across the sky, streaking down. Zordon's destruction order was about to be completed. The planet would survive. The Power Rangers would not.

"We will all die together, Rita," he said.

"NOOOOOOOOOOOOOOO!!!!!!!" Rita screamed.

Zordon took advantage of her distraction. Diving over the hole in the ground, he protected the coins with his own exposed body. Zordon felt the ground heave with the meteor's impact. He looked up.

The blast wave from the collision rolled over the landscape, destroying rocks, trees, the saurian animals . . . everything in its path. In the last moment before his annihilation, Zordon saw the blast fling Rita far away into the burning sky over the ocean. He had done the right thing.

CHAPTER ONE

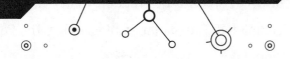

It was Prank Night in the town of Angel Grove, and Jason Scott had put some serious thought into what he ought to do: *Get a cow into the Montgomery High locker room and leave it there as a surprise for their first-period gym class tomorrow.* A little message from their crosstown rivals at Angel Grove High, where Jason was about to start his fourth year of football and . . . well, pretty much football. It would be legendary.

But the cow didn't seem to want to go into the locker room. It mooed loudly as Damo and Hawkeye, two of Jason's pals, braced themselves against its haunches.

"You know me," Damo was saying. "I never question

your pranks, you're the master . . . But we coulda just toilet-papered their sign like the seniors did last year. Why'd we steal a cow?"

"We borrowed this cow," Jason corrected him. "We are not thieves."

"We just tore the door off the locker room," Hawkeye pointed out.

Okay, maybe vandals. But not thieves, Jason thought. "Hawkeye, stay here," he said. "Be the lookout. Damo, pull yourself together." He patted the cow's flank. "Beefcake . . . time to be a winner."

They got the cow into the locker room. It mooed in the darkness and for some reason, the absurdity of the whole situation cracked both Jason and Damo up. The cow kept mooing, and they kept laughing, and then Hawkeye charged in. "COPS!!! THE COPS ARE COMING!!!!"

All three of them ran for the exit.

"Beefcake, I'm really sorry!" Jason said to the cow as he and the others ran out of the locker room.

Eventually, Beefcake started to follow them.

By the time Jason got to his truck and jammed it into reverse, one of the cops had cut him off. The truck slammed hard into the cop car. *Uh-oh*, Jason thought. Not cool. The only way out was . . . well, onto the lawn.

He gunned the truck over the curb and across the lawn, skidding around Beefcake. Jason rammed the truck through a fence, and the truck dropped hard down an embankment onto the road that cut behind Montgomery. The cops were still behind him. He made a sharp turn onto a side road and cut his headlights. In his rearview mirror he saw them go screaming by. He'd lost them. Nice!

He flipped his headlights back on, hitting the gas again . . . and framed in the headlights he saw a plumbing van backing out of a driveway in front of him.

Jason swerved around the van, but his truck plowed into a parked car at an angle. It rolled over a couple of times and skidded to a halt upside down. The impact stunned him for a moment, but pretty quickly he started to feel pain. A lot of pain, mostly coming from his knee. Even hanging upside down in the darkness, he could tell it didn't look right. Something told him it was going to be a while before he stepped foot on a football field again.

It was only supposed to be a prank, he thought. *Man, how did it go so wrong?*

CHAPTER TWO

Three weeks later, Jason sat in the passenger seat of his dad's truck, a beat-up old half-ton with a bed full of fishing gear and a cab full of old coffee cups. Sam Scott pulled up in front of Angel Grove High School and shook his head at the sight of the house arrest ankle bracelet on Jason's left leg.

"I don't think we'll ever understand each other," he said. "Just when I thought you'd done the dumbest thing you could possibly do, you find something dumber and you do it."

"Thank you," Jason said.

"I promise you, this is not the moment to joke around," his father said. Jason quieted down. You could only push Sam Scott so far. "I know you think it's noble that you didn't rat out your friends."

"I acted alone," Jason replied. "Beefcake and I had a connection."

"Yeah, that's funny. You know what's not funny?" His father paused, looking for some kind of reaction. "This was supposed to be your season! I had scouts coming to every game. You coulda written your own ticket. Now it's all gone. Now you gotta come here every Saturday for the rest of the year just to graduate. With all the other weirdos and criminals."

For the first time since they'd left the house, father and son looked each other in the eye. "Like you said," Jason said after a moment. "We'll never understand each other."

His father reached across him and opened the door. Nothing more to say. Jason got out, his right leg stiff and sore in the knee brace. He was a long way from healed.

Several parking spaces over, Kimberly Hart sat texting in the back of her father's car. Both of her parents were in the front seat. "This could've ended with far worse than Saturday detention," her father said.

"At least we can all agree on that," her mother added.

Kimberly looked up from her phone. "I didn't take that picture of Amanda Clark."

"You punched a boy in the face," her mother said.

"Okay, I did that," Kimberly admitted. "But he disrespected me." She didn't want to tell them how. Well, she did, but she couldn't.

"You knocked out his tooth," her father said. He was using his this-is-serious-young-lady voice.

"They put it back," Kimberly said. She could see her dad starting to get more upset and she cut him off before he could get going. "Nobody understands what actually happened!"

"Then explain it to us," her mother said.

She wanted to. God, she wanted to. It wasn't fair. But no. She couldn't. No matter how bad things got, Kimberly wasn't going to be a snitch.

"Pick me up later," she said, and got out of the car.

Jason walked slowly down the hall toward the detention classroom, favoring his injured leg. The brace helped a lot, but it was still weak and sore. He stopped to get a drink, looked up, and saw his own framed jersey: SCOTT 11. A reminder of what he'd lost by being stupid. He turned away from it and saw Kimberly Hart, one of Angel Grove's queen bees. Not the kind who just wanted to be on the arm of the football star, either. Self-possessed, beautiful, a force of nature. She blew by him, intent on her phone. Girls like Kimberly Hart didn't have time for him.

Someone mooed when he walked into the classroom. Everyone laughed. Jason played it off, ignoring the scorn from all the misfit losers who populated Saturday detention. Except for Kimberly Hart, who was in the back of the room, texting away.

Closer to Jason, Billy Cranston was arranging his colored pencils and making some kind of marks on a map. Strange kid, Billy. Another kid whose name Jason didn't know swaggered past Billy and knocked the pencils off his desk. "You're a freak," he said, leaning over Billy. "We've been watching you play with these pencils every week. It drives me crazy. Are you crazy? What if there was an extra one?"

He held up one of the pencils and snapped it in half. Billy twitched but tried to keep himself together. The bully held up another pencil and was about to snap it, too, when Jason had had enough.

In two steps he was in the kid's face. The class got dead quiet. "How old are you, five?" Jason shoved him away. "Hi, I'm Jason, this is my first time here. It's exciting. And you must be the bully—the bully of detention? How dumb can you be?"

The bully took a swing at Jason, but Jason saw it coming a mile away. He flicked the punch away with a simple high block, making it look even easier than it was. Another swing, another block. Neither punch came within a foot of landing. The kid hesitated. He had to keep fighting or he would look like an idiot. Jason solved the problem for him by slapping him square in the face.

Amazed, the kid said, "Did you just *slap* me?"

Jason nodded. "I did. Weird, right?" He stepped up to the kid, making sure everyone in the room saw what was happening. "I'm gonna be here every week for what seems like the rest of my life and I'm sure you are, too. Let's make a deal." He tapped his own chest and then pointed at the terrified geek with his pencils. "Don't sit near me or him, and we'll be okay."

Trying to save face, the defeated bully held Jason's stare for a moment before taking a seat in the back corner. Billy Cranston was grinning. Some of the other kids seemed to have enjoyed the show, too—including, Jason noticed, Kimberly Hart.

The detention teacher rolled through the door then, trying to assert order. "Okay. So. Approved homework or work on the *Better Choices* workbook. These should be out and in progress. And good morning."

Kimberly looked at something interesting on her phone, then stood. "I have to go to the ladies' room."

The teacher lifted a hand, but Kimberly ignored him just like she'd ignored Jason.

She went into the bathroom expecting to see Harper and Amanda, her friends who had been texting her, but the bathroom was silent. Kimberly was already on an emotional knife-edge. Her problems with Harper and Amanda kept her up at night, and now she thought it might all be taken care of . . . maybe? She didn't really know where she stood. And she wasn't going to find out in an empty bathroom.

Then the two girls popped out of one of the stalls, laughing. Kimberly joined in. Like her, Amanda and Harper were queen bees. They liked to dress alike, they exchanged tips on hairstyles and social currents at Angel Grove, and they were the heart of the cheerleading squad. It was their school, really.

"So this is where you come every Saturday instead of practice?" Amanda needled Kimberly. "Tragic."

"This must suck," Harper added. She spent a lot of time echoing what Amanda said.

"It does," Kimberly admitted. She was playing along to ease the tension, still not completely sure how this conversation was going to go.

Amanda smirked. "Then you shouldn't have sent Ty that picture of me."

"That's not exactly how it happened," Kimberly said.

"He's a liar." Amanda knew this. Why did Kimberly keep having to explain it?

"You punched his tooth out," Harper said.

God, it was annoying to keep hearing about that. "They put it back!"

"Details, details," Amanda said. "Truth is, for whatever reason, you went after me."

"You know there's way more to the story," Kimberly said.

Abruptly, Amanda's tone changed. "Water under the bridge now. Let's move on."

Kimberly couldn't believe it. "Really? Thank God." Relief crested in her like a wave, a physical feeling in her chest.

"We're moving on . . . without you." The wave crashed down, and Kimberly had the awful empty feeling in her stomach that came when someone made a fool of you.

"Cutting you out," Harper added. "Literally." She showed Kimberly a picture of all three girls at a party, looking happy and cool together. In Harper's other hand was a pair of scissors. She cut Kimberly out of the picture.

"Unfriended, unfollowed, don't text me," Amanda said.

"You can show up for cheer practice if you want," Harper said. "But I wouldn't." She pinned the mutilated photo to the bathroom wall with the scissors, and the two girls left without looking back.

Kimberly took a long look at the picture, and at her reflection next to it in the big bathroom mirror. Suddenly she hated what she saw, hated the way she'd let herself think that being part of that little clique was so important that she would—

No, she wasn't going to think about that. She was cut out? *Well, fine,* she thought. *Then it's time for some changes.*

She pulled the scissors out of the wall and ran her finger along one of the blades. They were nice and sharp. She pulled a fistful of her hair away from her head and cut it off. Then she cut a big hunk out of the other side. Oh, it felt good. She didn't have to be the same as them. She didn't have to worry about what anyone thought anymore. Kimberly's hair fell into the sink and onto the floor and she didn't care. She was going to be someone new.

Jason did a double take when Kimberly came back into the detention classroom. The haircut was one thing, but the expression on her face—tough, daring, strong—made her look like she could be fronting a punk band. The room erupted in yells and whistles. Kimberly looked around, soaking it all up. Jason couldn't take his eyes off her. Man, he'd liked her before, but now . . . he liked her a lot. A whole lot.

This new Kimberly distracted Jason for the rest of detention, and he was still watching her as they walked back outside. Her parents picked her up and freaked out at her haircut. Jason didn't even notice the pencil-collecting nerd next to him until he spoke. "Thank you for that in there."

Jason barely glanced at him. "No worries. I hate guys like that."

"Yeah, for sure. So, we should hang out. Not that we

have to, but tonight we should."

Jason wrestled with the nerd's name for a bit. Ah. Billy Cranston. "Billy. I would, honestly, hang out with you, but I have a date every night." Jason lifted his pant leg to show the ankle bracelet. Billy nodded, understanding.

Then Jason started walking off, and Billy called after him. "Wait! Just wait. Come back." Jason turned and took a step back. "I'm not really expecting to hang out with you. I'd like to get somewhere tonight and I need some help. It's important."

"Okay, Billy," Jason said. "I hear you, relax. But as I told you, I have . . ." He lifted his pant leg again.

"I can fix that," Billy said. "I know how to trick the SIM card. I have tools."

Well, Jason thought. *That's interesting.* "I have to be in my house before seven."

"If you come to my house tonight before seven, I can fix it." Billy saw Jason wasn't convinced. "I also have a car . . . well, access to a car . . . so if you decide to help me, you could have the car for a few hours. Just gotta pick me up," Billy said. He started to walk away. "Come anytime before seven."

Access to a car, Jason thought. *That might even be worth dealing with Billy Cranston's weirdness.*

CHAPTER THREE

It was a fine day to go train surfing, and Zack wasn't going to miss his chance.

He hopped the freight train before it picked up too much speed and climbed up onto the roof of a boxcar. Snowboarding goggles covered most of his face, and he kept his hoodie pulled down tight, too. Once he was up on the train, he held out a selfie stick and turned a complete circle.

"Greetings, followers!" he said, shouting over the noise of the train and the wind. "I'm copping a free ride on the rails today! If you dig it, subscribe to my channel. Click on the link below. Today's quote comes from Confucius. He was an old Chinese dude who knew some stuff. He said, 'Our greatest glory is not in never falling, but in rising every time we fall . . .'"

He threw a peace sign at the camera, closed the selfie stick, and put it in his backpack. Then he took out his phone—but dropped it.

It slid along the top of the car as Zack fumbled after it. Just as it came to a stop and he was about to get it, it buzzed with an incoming text message and bounced off the train!

Zack lunged after it, barely hanging on—and then the train hooked a tight turn, and he went over the side.

He caught a ladder with one hand, still holding his phone with the other. Who was the message from? He swiped to see. Then he grinned, raised the camera to take a selfie—

And saw a telephone pole heading toward him as the train roared along the tracks at sixty miles an hour. Whoa!

Zack jackknifed back up onto the top of the train, ruining the selfie but missing the telephone pole by inches. When he landed on the roof of the boxcar again, he was smiling. This was going to be a great day.

He was almost to the old mine site where the train would slow down enough for him to hop off. Maybe the weird girl would be out there again today.

CHAPTER FOUR

When he got home from detention, Jason dug around in the fridge for leftovers. Pulling out a half-eaten sandwich, he sniffed it for freshness. Shutting the door, he saw a picture of himself. A newspaper clipping, with the headline ANGEL GROVE'S GOLDEN BOY.

His dad walked into the kitchen and, without saying a word, started to wash his hands.

The awkward silence built until Jason couldn't take it anymore. He stormed out of the kitchen and headed to the safety of his bedroom.

He flopped down onto his bed, trying very hard to control his anger. It was getting harder by the day. His dad didn't understand him. All Sam Scott wanted was his football star. It was like Jason didn't exist unless he was on the field.

Coming from the kitchen, Jason could hear his parents' muffled voices, fighting over him again.

"Don't be so hard on him!" his mom said. "How do you think he feels walking around town now?"

"Well, how do you think I feel walking around town now?" his dad replied. "What's the plan, huh? What's he gonna do with his life? He could have been so much more."

Jason couldn't listen to this conversation again. He sat up and a grabbed a small baseball trophy from his dresser. Any joy or pride it once made him feel was gone. He snapped it in half, then jumped up.

The clock in his room read 6:22 p.m. Jason had to get out of there. Anywhere else would be better. But how? His truck was either still in the impound lot or at the junkyard by now. And he wasn't going to be walking anywhere. He needed wheels.

Billy Cranston had wheels.

Weird situation, Jason thought. He'd never spoken to

Billy before that day. Now Billy was offering him freedom from the bracelet, and a car . . . in return for what?

Only one way to find out.

Three minutes later he was in the garage pumping up the back tire of his old bike. One minute after that he was pedaling hard on the way to Billy Cranston's house, trying to ignore the ache in his knee. He was going to be free again if it killed him.

CHAPTER FIVE

Jason made it all the way across town to Billy Cranston's house in twenty-five minutes flat. Pretty good, considering his knee was killing him the whole way. Billy's mom opened the door and freaked out. "Oh . . . my . . . God. Jason Scott." She turned to yell up the stairs. "Billy! Jason Scott is here!"

Over her shoulder, Jason saw a clock with a cat face. It was nearly 7:00 p.m. "Billy's room upstairs?" he asked. When Mrs. Cranston nodded, he limped up the stairs as fast as he could and barged through the nearest closed door. Sure enough, it was Billy's room. Jason slammed the door and pulled up his pant leg. A light on the bracelet was flashing. If it was still flashing at 7:00 p.m.,

Jason would be in big trouble. "Dude," he said.

"Six fifty-six," Billy said. "I know. Four minutes to go. Grab that chair!" Jason slid a chair over to a table where Billy was rooting around in a heap of weird electronics and stuff. He dug a tube of wire mesh, closed at one end, out of the junk in the closet. "Here! Put your foot in this."

"What is it?"

"A Faraday cage. Sort of. It will block the cell signal. I hope . . ."

Jason put his foot in as the bracelet started beeping. "That's the three-minute warning," he said.

Billy was distracted. "My dad's dead now. He's been dead seven years, four months, and two days."

"Uh-huh." The beeping was faster now. "Billy, it's almost—"

Billy pried the SIM card out of the ankle bracelet. "He worked at the mine. We found objects together. It was awesome." He slotted the SIM card into his computer and tapped away. "You still live at forty-four fifty-five Old Wharf? My dad and I both liked old stuff, history . . . Do you watch—?"

"Dude, the signal's gonna go off!" Jason said, nearly shouting.

Billy slipped the SIM card back into the bracelet and pulled away the mesh. The red light turned green. The beeping stopped. Jason realized he'd been holding his breath. "Yes?"

Billy nodded. "Yes!"

Jason couldn't help it. He gave weird Billy Cranston a big hug and said, "Thank you." Billy tensed up and wouldn't look him in the eye. He just nodded and then replied quietly, "Can you stop touching me now?"

Jason nodded to Billy's mother on his way back out the door. In the driveway were a sporty little car and a boring minivan. Jason waited next to the sports coupe. He could already hear its engine rumbling to life, feel the way its suspension would stiffen up on tight curves . . . Jason loved to drive, and this was the kind of car that made driving fun.

But when Billy came outside, he said, "We're taking the van." Before Jason could protest, Billy pointed to a footlocker near the garage door. "Can you help me?"

They got the footlocker into the van, and Billy handed Jason the keys. "You can drive." *At least I've got that going for me*, Jason thought.

Billy smiled and tapped a seashell hanging from the rearview mirror. "Gotta swing the shell. Always gotta swing the shell for luck. Let's roll."

CHAPTER SIX

Twenty minutes later, they were easing the minivan over a railroad crossing. A sign at the crossing said CASCADIA GOLD MINE—AUTHORIZED VEHICLES ONLY. "Keep driving," Billy said. The sun was going down when they got to the end of an abandoned road, high in the hills. Billy jumped out and pulled a map from his pocket. "This is it. Me and my dad's secret spot to find stuff. We're going around back. I'm gonna need your help."

Jason was nervous. They could get in trouble out here, and if anyone found out about the bracelet . . . "Listen, man, the deal was I drop you somewhere and I get the van for a few hours. You didn't say we were breaking into the mine. I can't get arrested again."

Billy didn't look up from the map. "You stole a cow and evaded police."

"I borrowed that cow," Jason corrected him. "He was unharmed."

Billy had seen something on the map. "Grab the locker," he said.

They hauled the footlocker along the side of the mountain as the sun set. Then they paused to look out over the huge quarry near the older mine shafts that cut deep into the mountain. "They're gonna blow this whole thing, y'know?" Billy said. "It'll be gone in a week. Makes me sad."

"Billy," Jason said. "Can I be honest? This is weird. We don't know each other at all, I don't know what we're doing, and you seem kinda—"

"I need to let you know something," Billy said. "I'm on the spectrum."

No kidding, Jason thought. He didn't want Billy to be nervous, so he tried to lighten things up. "Is that a workout program? Like Tae Bo?"

"It's a diagnosis," Billy said seriously.

So much for lightening things up. "I know. It was a joke. I was kidding."

"I didn't get the joke," Billy said. He was very earnest. "That's the thing. My brain doesn't work the same way yours does."

"Consider that a good thing," Jason said.

"See, I'm not so good at sarcasm, or humor—but I can remember things. Anything. Everything. But I communicate strangely and—"

"Billy, let me stop you," Jason said. The conversation was weirding him out, and he could tell Billy was talking about it because he felt like he had to. But he didn't have to. Jason didn't care. "We're cool."

"People get frustrated with me," Billy said. "Don't get frustrated with me. If you get frustrated with me . . . let me know. Just say—"

"You're frustrating me," Jason said.

That brought Billy up short. "I am right now?"

"No. I was finishing your sentence," Jason said. He reminded himself to be calm and literal—two things that weren't always easy for Jason Scott. "If you frustrate me,

I will let you know. We're cool."

"We're cool?"

"Yes. Let's not have a frustrating conversation about frustration."

Billy nodded. He squatted in front of the footlocker and got out a flashlight. "It will be dark when you come back," he said, holding it out toward Jason. "We can find each other—"

"Bye, Billy," Jason said, cutting him off.

Billy just looked up, replied, "Okay!" and went back to work.

Jason had just gotten to the van when he heard some music in the distance. Who else would be out here? He went to find out and got a big surprise.

Kimberly Hart stood on a stone ledge off the trail, just stepping out of her jeans. *Whoa,* Jason thought. Before he could figure out what she was doing, she dove backward off the ledge.

The spring was a good distance below. Jason heard the splash before he got to the ledge.

"Hey!" he shouted. She didn't come up.

"Kim! Kimberly!" His voice echoed off the rocks.

She still didn't come up. He had to do something.

Jason kicked off his shoes and looked for a good place to dive in after her. Then he heard her say, "Strange to hear you say my name."

He spun around to see her climbing up onto the ledge from another direction. When she got all the way up, she wrapped herself in a towel.

"What?" Jason said. It was turning out to be a very weird day.

"I said, it was strange to hear you say my name. Like we knew each other."

"We know each other," Jason said.

"We know who each other *are*," she corrected him. "But we don't know each other."

"I know you used to date Ty Fleming."

"Then you know I punched his tooth out."

Jason grinned at her. "I know they put it back."

She tried not to return his smile.

They headed back through the trees together toward

the minivan. Jason had decided he wouldn't take off on Billy. Especially not if Kimberly was out here.

"What are you doing up here?" she asked as they walked. "Did you follow me?"

"I came with Billy."

"Cranston? Weird. But I've seen him here before. My house is on the other side of the mountain. I hike these trails sometimes. Clear my head." They reached an overlook where they could see all the way to the ocean. "And I stare down at Angel Grove and wonder how such a small town could cause me such misery."

Jason couldn't help it. He laughed.

"That's funny?" Kimberly had a dangerous look in her eyes.

"I feel the same way," Jason said.

"Yeah," she said. "Jason Scott, star quarterback, crashes and burns. Destroys his career and destroys our season. Go, Tigers!"

Jason decided to believe she was on his side. "Now I walk around town and everyone is looking at me like I ran over their dog."

"I could leave here," Kimberly mused. "You know? Just go."

Now they were very close. "So let's go," Jason said.

"What?" She took a step back. "You'd never do it."

"Try me."

"You and me? You got a car?"

"I have a van," Jason said. *Well, access to a van*, he thought.

"Seriously? A van? Be creepier."

"It's not that kind of van."

She rolled her eyes. "Every van is that kind of van."

"Let's go," Jason said. He nodded back down the trail, where the minivan was parked.

"Are you daring me? Because I'll go." They stared at each other for a long moment, feeling something start to crackle between them. "This isn't—I don't know what you're thinking," she added.

Kimberly had never expected Jason Scott to be charming. Sometimes people were full of surprises. She was just starting to crack a smile when something exploded over near the mine.

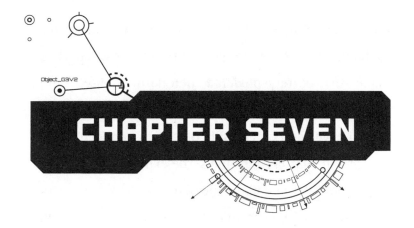

CHAPTER SEVEN

Zack was sitting on an abandoned boxcar chowing down on a pizza and looking through binoculars at one of the other kids who came out to the Cascadia property to hide out from the world. He'd seen her around school but he didn't know her name. Lots of black, hard stares. Tough girl. She was doing some kind of yoga thing on the edge of a cliff. When he heard the explosion he swung the binoculars around and spotted the source. Then he took off running.

Billy staggered to his feet just as Jason came running

up . . . with Kimberly Hart. What was she doing here? He hadn't meant for the explosion to be that big. He'd made the battery-powered detonator himself and counted the steps back down the old mine passage. It should have been far enough. But when he touched the wires to the battery terminals, the explosion was, wow, a lot bigger than he had expected.

"Oh, man!" he shouted. "That really rung my bell! Wow!"

Jason was glad to see Billy was okay. Another kid came running from down the road and grabbed Billy by the jacket. "What are you doin', dude?"

"I've been digging up here for many years!" Billy yelled.

Jason got the other kid's hands off Billy's coat. His name was Zack, wasn't it? Jason was pretty sure that was it. "Easy, guy," he said. "Let's sort this out."

Zack shoved him away. "I've seen him up here before, diggin' around, whatever. Some of us camp out up here on the downlow, and this dude cannot be blasting stuff!"

"I just wanted to go a little deeper!" Billy yelled. "Maybe I went too deep!"

Jason got his attention. "Billy, you don't have to yell. We can hear you, okay?"

"Okay!" Billy yelled.

"Hey!" Someone else was yelling now, too. A girl none of them knew appeared from the same direction Zack had come from. "You guys looking to get busted? This is a restricted area!"

"Really, Einstein? Restricted?" Zack shot back. "As in, we shouldn't be standing on crazy rocks doing *Karate Kid* moves?" He did a mocking version of the crane pose from the movie. "I see you."

Billy had already moved away; he'd become distracted by something else. "Um, guys," he said, quieter now.

"Or camping out on an old train?" the girl said, jousting with Zack. "I see you, too, homeboy."

Jason looked back and forth between the two of them. He was starting to realize there were a lot of people at Angel Grove High that he didn't know.

"Oh, no," Billy said from behind them. A moment later, the whole rock face on that side of the hill collapsed, knocking them all over and covering them with dust. They got to their feet, unharmed but coughing and sneezing. "Whoa," Billy said.

All of them saw it at once. The collapse had exposed a wall of black obsidian, like glass. It was cracked in spots, maybe from the explosion Billy had set off. And inside, there were . . . some kind of round objects . . .

"I've never seen glass like this before," Billy said.

Zack grabbed an old pickax and stepped toward the glass wall.

The others tried to stop him, but he wouldn't listen. He struck that glass wall as hard as he could. One of the round things fell out at Billy's feet. Zack smashed away and the rest of them fell out.

"It's like a stone or coin or something," Billy said as he picked it up.

They all gathered to take a look. Jason thought they did look like coins. The one in Billy's hand was flickering with a deep blue light. Were they battery-powered?

How had they gotten into the rocks? Man, they were cool. He looked more closely at the one Billy held. A rocky crust covered part of it. Through that, light and colors swirled on its surface. Was that a pattern? It was hard to tell through the crust, but it didn't look like a machine. How was it glowing like that? Jason had never seen anything like it.

Billy was practically glowing himself, with delight and pride. "My dad always knew the best spots."

"We all found them," Zack said. "And if they're worth money—"

"No, *he* found them," Jason said, nodding at Billy. "Chill out."

Then Kimberly said, "Do you hear that?"

All of them did. Sirens, getting closer.

"Mine security!" Zack said.

They ran in different directions. Jason got to the van and got it started as Billy piled in. A mine security van and two ATVs were chasing around after the other three kids. Jason gunned the van down the sloping dirt road. "You gonna leave the others?" Billy shouted.

He hauled the van around in a one-eighty and nearly collided with one of the ATVs. The girls were running down the path that ran parallel to the road. Jason caught Billy's eye and nodded at the steering wheel. "You drive!" He let the wheel go and jumped into the back of the van.

"I don't really drive!" Billy shouted back.

"Then don't really drive a little closer to the edge of the road so I can pull them in!"

The van swerved around as Billy got control. Well, sort of. Jason threw the sliding door open. "Come on! Get in!" he shouted at the girls. They ran faster. He pulled them in, and all three of them spilled onto the seat.

"What about the other guy?" Billy shouted.

Jason looked at the girls. They looked at him. Then they all shouted, "Just go!" Zack could take care of himself.

"Downhill!" Jason yelled. "Just drive to the lights! Go!" Jason climbed into the front passenger seat and looked ahead. "Keep going! We're almost out—look, there's the road and the railroad crossing!"

The crossing lights on the tracks flashed red and the crossing gate was coming down to block the road. "Guys, there's a train," Kimberly said nervously. They could all see it coming.

"Keep going," Jason said. "We got it." At least he thought they did.

A second later, out of nowhere, Zack slammed down onto the windshield and scrambled to hold on to the hood. All of them were screaming at each other. Jason ripped open the side door again and reached to get a grip on Zack. Kimberly helped. They all fell onto the backseat again. "Are you crazy?" Jason shouted.

Zack was grinning. "Yes, I am!"

Billy kept his foot on the gas. They were getting closer to the crossing. "We got it, we got it, we got it," Jason said over and over again. The train was coming fast, but they would make it. Sure they would. The van barreled closer to the crossing. Jason leaned forward in his seat like he could push the van to go faster. It was going to be close. Real close . . .

Too close, he realized, too late to do anything about it. The train was right on them, blaring its horn. Glare from its headlight filled the inside of the van. They crashed through the crossing gate, splintering its wooden arms—and a split second later, the train crashed into them.

CHAPTER EIGHT

Object_43H1

Object_T1349

The *Sleep Robber* pitched and rolled in a heavy sea. "Jake! Pull up the nets!" Sam Scott shouted over the rising storm. The weather had changed fast, and they needed to get out of there before the nets fouled and they lost their catch.

The nets rose out of the water, wriggling with fish that gleamed in the boat's spotlights. The winch boom swung over the deck and released the nets. Their catch flopped into the hold. Something in the middle of the pile of fish hit the deck with a heavy thud. It was hard to see what it was until they got closer.

"What is that?" Sam asked.

Inside the boat's hold there seemed to be some kind

of frozen body. A faint green glow appeared. Then its eyes burst open.

Jason woke up in the morning, stretched—and remembered the chase. Remembered the train!

He jumped out of bed. His window was open. He must have come in that way. But how—? He looked down at himself. Everything was intact. He felt okay. He felt great, in fact. His knee didn't hurt at all. But the train . . .

The red coin from the glass wall in the hillside was in his jeans. How had it gotten there? He didn't even remember picking it up. Jason turned it over in his hands. The red glow flowed around to the other side of it, almost like it was reacting to his presence.

Something about it spooked him. He tucked it into his desk drawer and headed for the bathroom. At least everything in there was normal . . . until Jason turned on the water to wash up and he saw the coin out of the corner of his eye. It was sitting on the corner of the sink. How—?

I just put it in my desk, Jason thought. *It's like the thing is following me . . .*

No. On top of everything else, that idea was too much. Jason ducked over the toilet and threw up, just from the stress and weirdness of it all. Getting his balance, he caught the edge of the sink—and the corner of it snapped off in his hand. He looked at the broken piece of ceramic. How was that possible? How was any of it possible?

Kimberly looked in the mirror, uneasy from strange dreams. Or were they memories? No, they couldn't be. Her phone chimed with text messages. She looked down to swipe them away. The gold-edged coin with its pink pattern was next to her phone. Her phone kept chiming. Finally, she looked at one of the messages. It was a picture of Amanda, Harper, and another girl sticking their tongues out. They wanted to rub her face in it. Hurt and angry, Kimberly squeezed the phone tight. She didn't know she was doing it until it snapped in her hand. Shards of the glass screen fell to the floor.

Amazed, she looked at what she'd done. Then she squeezed the phone harder, crumpling it into a tiny ball of electronics and twisted metal.

Whoa, Kimberly thought. She was a little bit frightened. But at the same time, she was a whole lot excited.

Billy Cranston shot out of bed when his alarm went off, and fell over, feet tangled in his sheets. He turned off his alarm and looked around. When he saw himself in the mirror, he was stunned. He still wore the clothes from yesterday, and he was still covered in dirt from the explosion. His hair was dirty and tangled. Was he remembering it right? The black glass wall, the train . . .

The coin. There was that coin on his nightstand. He picked it up and looked at it. There was something about it, something weird, that blue pattern inside the encrusted gold edge. He decided he'd better hide it. He pulled on his closet door, forgetting it was stuck. It came loose and sailed across the room, crashing off his desk and breaking his window.

"Billy!" his mother called from downstairs. "What's happening in there?"

Billy shoved the door back onto its track. He had no idea how to answer her. What was happening in here? How was he alive? And when had he gotten so strong?

CHAPTER NINE

Billy was feeling pretty good about himself when he got to school on Monday. Things were weird, but that was fantastic! As he reached up to get a book from the top shelf of his locker, somebody knocked it out of his hand. Billy turned and saw the bully from detention. "Where's your bodyguard?" he sneered. He grabbed Billy's wrist.

"What are you doing?" Billy asked. He wasn't afraid. A little nervous, maybe, the way he always got in social situations, but he'd walked away from a train crash. He wasn't scared the way he used to be.

"I'm gonna snap your wrist," the bully said.

He leaned on Billy's wrist with all his weight, and Billy just stared at him. Then he let go. People were watching.

The bully got desperate. He reared back and head-butted Billy . . . but Billy didn't even move, and the bully pitched straight over backward like he'd gone headfirst into a brick wall. He lay flat on his back, right in front of a whole hallway full of Angel Grove students.

Someone in the crowd said, "Billy Cranston just knocked Colt Wallace out cold. Bam, dude. Bam."

Billy closed his locker. *So that's the bully's name,* he thought. He walked down the hall and the sea of kids parted to let him through. Billy couldn't help but grin.

At lunch, Billy Cranston was suddenly a legend amid Angel Grove's outcasts and freaks. They all wanted to hear the story, and he enjoyed telling it. "I said, 'Hey, I'm not a violent man. But if you must come at me . . . come at me, bro.'"

Another kid walked up, offered Billy a fist bump, and said, "Down he goes!"

Everyone fell silent as Kimberly Hart suddenly appeared among them. It was like a visit from a goddess. Billy tried to stay casual. "Oh, hey. Kimberly Hart."

"Billy, we need to talk," she said, and walked away again.

Billy looked around at his friends' stunned faces. He started to say something, then just smiled. As he hurried after Kimberly, he heard one of them say, "Since when does he know Kimberly Hart?"

"Billy's awesome."

His smile got bigger.

Kimberly and Billy headed down to the end of the service counter, where steam and dirty dishes kept everyone else away.

"Hey," Kimberly said. "Do you feel weird?"

"Weirder than usual?"

She nodded. "Yeah. Different."

He nodded back. Kimberly put her coin down on the counter. Billy put his next to it. Jason appeared from behind them and added his. *Some of the crusty, fossilized stuff has fallen off,* Billy thought. *The patterns in them are really interesting.*

"Listen, we know something happened up there,"

Jason said. "I'm not the same."

"Me neither—I'm strong," Billy said. He still couldn't believe it.

"How strong?" Kimberly asked.

Billy searched for the right word. "Insanely strong."

"I feel like we need to go back up there," Kimberly said.

They were looking at each other, thinking it over, when they heard a whirring noise. The three coins hovered a few inches above the counter's surface. Jason slapped them back down onto the counter and held them there. He could feel the counter beginning to overheat. Suddenly some soda cans that were lined up on the other end exploded.

The three new friends—if that's what they were—locked eyes.

"We're going back there today," Jason said.

Officer Meinen had been with the Angel Grove Police Department for seven years. Long enough to see some weird stuff. But this was the weirdest, for sure. After he interviewed Sam Scott and his crew on the *Sleep Robber*, he let them go and started a careful investigation of the scene. First, he looked over the deceased without touching her. She looked frozen. That was weird all by itself. She was in water. How was she frozen? Plus, her body was bent in strange ways, like some huge force had crushed her into that position. And the weirdest thing of all was that she seemed . . . well, something about her seemed old, but Meinen didn't know what. He noticed something stuck to the woman's hand. It was perfectly round. Some kind of disk, or coin. He bent down to reach for it.

At the same time, she reached up for him.

CHAPTER TEN

A winch pulled Billy's mother's van up onto a flatbed truck as they passed by in Kimberly's BMW. The wreckage was so crushed and twisted, no one inside could have survived the impact. Jason noticed Billy clutched his coin in one hand.

"We should keep going," Kimberly said as they continued on.

When they got to the blast site, they saw Zack was already there, poking around in the hole in the glass wall.

"Find anything interesting?" Jason called.

Zack shook his head. "But if I do, I'm keeping it."

"We know why you're here," Kimberly said. She didn't feel like dealing with his tough-guy pose.

"Oh yeah?" Zack said. "Did you guys wake up surprised to be alive and jump over a house?"

"Yes," Billy said. "No. Kind of. Things are different. We're different."

Kimberly walked over to the glass wall. "You're Zack, right?" she asked.

"Yup."

"You still go to Angel Grove?" Jason honestly didn't know.

Zack looked away. "Sometimes."

There is some kind of trouble there, Jason thought. A family thing. But he wasn't going to ask.

"The other girl was here," Zack added. "About an hour ago. She didn't want her coin, and I told her I would gladly take it. She didn't love that idea."

Billy pointed up and over Zack's head. "You mean that girl right there?"

They all turned to see her looking down from the top of the rocks.

"Hey," Jason called. "It's us. Come on down." She took a step back. "We should all talk about this," he said, taking a step in her direction.

She took off running, Zack following close behind.

Kimberly held up a hand as Jason started to go after her. "Let me handle this," she said, sprinting off. Soon she overtook Zack. Trini reached the rock wall first and scaled it like she was a spider. After a moment, the rest of them followed.

CHAPTER ELEVEN

Object_T1349

Kimberly got to the top of the rock formation and saw the girl—what was her name, anyway?—at the edge of a deep chasm. On the other side of the drop was another sloping rock ledge. "Stop," Kimberly said. "Just talk to me." The girl turned to face her. "You have a coin. We have a coin," Kimberly said. She took a step forward. "We should talk about this. I mean, we don't—"

Then the girl jumped. She made it all the way across the chasm with room to spare, and landed in a crouch on the other side. Zack had just gotten to the top of the rock. He saw the girl land and shouted, "You're crazy!" With a big grin he added, "But so am I!"

"Whoa," Kimberly said. "Zack, wait . . ."

"No, I got this. I got this," he muttered, ignoring her. Then he launched himself across the chasm. He wasn't nearly as graceful as the girl. When he landed, he plowed into her and they both hit the ground.

"I got her! Just jump across!" he panted.

Kimberly looked at Jason. "Let's go. Jump with me."

Jason glanced over at Billy. "I'm gonna jump across with her, and then you jump."

He and Kimberly jumped. She landed and did a perfect cheerleader's roll. Jason crashed much like Zack had. Wincing with pain, he tried to reassure Billy. "No problem! Piece of cake! You got this! It's fun!"

"It's such a far jump . . . ," Billy muttered as the others joined in cheering him on.

He shook his head, like he was talking to himself— then he sprinted for the edge and jumped! He crashed into the lip and scrambled over. "I did it! I did it!" he shouted, hands up and dancing around. Jason clapped and smiled—and then Billy lost his balance and fell over the edge.

Jason ran to the edge and looked down. "Billy!"

No answer.

They all looked at each other.

"Did we just kill that dude?" Zack wondered. "What do we do?"

There was a moment of deathly quiet. Then they heard Billy's voice. "Hey, guys! You gotta jump down here! There's water! You gotta see this!"

With a broad smile, Zack turned to Jason. "See you down there. Bring the crazy girl," he said, and then he jumped.

His energy was contagious. Jason looked at Kimberly. "Come on, you guys, let's go!"

He jumped. The two girls stood next to each other, looking over the edge into the darkness. "This whole thing is insane," Kimberly said. She smiled at the other girl. "I'm Kimberly."

"I know who you are," the other girl said. "Everyone does. You know my name?"

Kimberly felt bad about it, but she didn't.

The girl studied Kimberly, a hard, judgmental stare. "My name's Trini, not that you'll remember it."

"Come on!" Jason's voice echoed up from the bottom of the chasm. "Jump!"

Trini started to leave. "Wait!" Kimberly said. "Trini. Can I get a sip of your water? I'm dying."

Trini looked at her water bottle. There was a little left. "Don't finish it," she said, and held the bottle out.

Kimberly took it. "Thanks." She put her other hand on Trini's shoulder. "And I'm really sorry."

"Sorry for what?" Trini asked—just as Kimberly got a grip on Trini's backpack and pulled her over the edge, into the abyss.

CHAPTER TWELVE

All five of them floated in the dark water. The only light came from a faint glow around each of the kids, each of them in a different color. Trini was trying to hide a smile. "Check out how we glow!" Jason said.

"I'm blue," Billy said as he scanned his body. "It's not my favorite color, but it's cool!"

"I'm black," Zack called out.

"No. You're not," Billy replied.

"I am!" Zack said.

Billy looked down into the water. "Hey guys, there's something down here. Follow me!"

He jackknifed under the water and they followed. At the bottom of the chasm was a mirrored surface. Billy reached out and touched his reflection. His hand pushed through it . . . then the rest of him went through. Jason, Kimberly, Trini, and Zack bumbled after, falling *through* the bottom of the water!

They landed in a cave, stunned and amazed at what they had just seen. Billy looked up. The ceiling of the cave was rippling water.

They walked slowly down the passage in the near-dark. "Do you hear that?" Kimberly looked around. There was a humming noise in the cave, but they couldn't tell where it was coming from. She turned on her phone flashlight.

Jason ran his hands along the cave walls. He found an opening. "C'mon, there's something out here."

Billy was the first one through. The humming was louder. The other four followed him, and what they saw amazed them even more than the watery ceiling.

"That's amazing!" said Billy.

They had come out into a larger cave, bigger than a football field. And smack in the middle of it, half buried in the ancient stone floor, was a spaceship. It was huge, silvery, and rounded, almost like it had been grown instead of built. The size of it . . . It seemed as big as an aircraft carrier down there in the cave. "This has probably been here for millions of years," Billy said. He pointed. "The rocks . . . they've grown around it."

Zack pointed, too. There was a portal up on the side of the ship. It looked like it was jammed half open. There was other damage to the ship, too, like it had crashed.

"I don't like this place," Kimberly said.

Then Jason noticed that his coin was glowing red. "Hey, guys!" he said. "Check this out!"

Suddenly the door to the spaceship opened all the way.

Jason and Kimberly looked at each other for a somber moment. "Okay," they said, and they all climbed up and went through the portal.

Inside was a huge open sphere. Dim lights glowed along the walls, but the size of the ship was scary. Anything could be in there.

"Are there, like . . . aliens here?" Zack whispered.

Jason turned to look at him. "Just be quiet, Zack."

Billy's voice was shaky. "Jason, is this real?! Are we really in a spaceship?"

"I think so," Jason said. "Just breathe." Billy was hyperventilating. He needed to calm down.

The girls caught up to them as Billy got himself together. "Hey, we've all seen enough here," Trini said. "We should go now?"

Zack reappeared from the shadows with a huge grin on his face. "We're gonna be famous!"

"What's wrong with you?" Kimberly snapped back. "We don't even know what this is yet."

Jason heard something. "Quiet!" He held up a hand. "There's someone here. Listen."

Looking up, they saw the tiles of the ceiling shifting and whirling into place. The ship seemed to be coming alive around them. Behind them, the portal suddenly latched closed.

"What's that?" Jason asked as he spun around. "What's going on?"

Billy looked at the closed portal. "The door," he called out.

"Oh my god," Kimberly cried. "There's no way out!"

Jason scanned the room and saw a walkway leading away from them. "Let's go!" he called out, and led the way.

Scared, they fled into the tunnel. They heard a strange metallic scraping, like a huge machine was grinding toward them. There was light coming from the same direction as the sound. A long shadow fell across the walkway. What was it? Now there was a weird kind of drilling sound . . . and all of a sudden Trini cried out, "It's got me!"

The others turned and saw her being dragged across the floor into the center of the enormous room.

"Dede, I'm coming," Zack mistakenly called to Trini as he ran after her.

The lights came up a little more, and they saw she was in the grip of a robot. It was about four feet tall, and sort of humanoid in shape. Even a little potbellied. It had glowing eyes on stalks sticking out from a disc-shaped head, and its limbs looked like they could extend and retract. It had stretched all the way out to get Trini, and dragged her back, without ever moving its feet.

"Hello," the robot said.

Zack charged it, and the robot smacked him across the room with its free arm. They all surrounded it.

"So happy you're here," it added.

"We'll kill you," Jason threatened.

"Kill me. Yeah, I wouldn't do that," the robot answered.

"There's five of us," Kimberly pointed out.

"Yes," the robot said. "I know. I have been waiting for you. Wait, where's the other one. One, two, three, four—there he is. Come here, buster!" It shot out an arm and dragged Zack back toward the group. "All of you."

"In a spaceship buried underground?" Billy asked. "How long have you been waiting?"

"Is today Monday?" the robot asked.

"Yeah," Billy replied.

"Then about sixty-five million years! Is that a long time?! I don't know." The robot looked them over. "You guys are young. This is not good."

There was only one reason the robot could have been expecting them, Jason thought. "This has to do with the coins?"

"Yes, the coins. The mysteries of the universe!" The robot got excited, talking faster and not making any sense. "I have so many questions! Did you find the coins or did the coins find you? Can you daydream at night? Do vegetarians eat animal crackers? If man evolved from monkeys, how come we still have monkeys?! Anyone? Don't answer that!"

It released Zack and Trini, then pointed past them. "Turn around. Proceed!"

CHAPTER THIRTEEN

"Let's focus on getting out of here," Kimberly said. "Stay together and when we see a chance . . ."

"We run," Trini finished.

"Okay," Jason agreed. "If we don't get a chance . . ."

"Then we kill it," Zack said.

The robot interrupted them. "You guys know I can hear every word you're saying, right?"

Looking around, they appeared to be in some kind of control room. In a smaller room off to the side and up a few steps there was a big pilot's chair surrounded by consoles. In the middle of the big room was a glowing blue sphere surrounded by five raised platforms. On each platform was a set of footprints.

"Please step into the footprints," the robot said.

None of them did. "Hey—question . . . What are you?" Billy asked.

"I'm Alpha 5, at your service." The robot looked at all of them.

"What?" Jason asked.

"He said he's Alpha 5," Billy replied as he stepped up to the platform.

As he placed his feet on the footprints, it acknowledged his presence. The others watched, waiting for something terrible to happen.

"You all must be in place for it to work," said Alpha 5. "Let's go."

Zack was next. He confidently strode over to his set of footprints. The others looked at each other before moving.

"Take your time, guys," Alpha 5 continued. "I've only been here for sixty-five million years. Why do you guys keep looking at each other? Is that some sort of human thing?"

The rest of them stepped on, Jason last. As his feet

met the prints, a deep thrum rolled through the ship and lights around the room blazed to life. The kids ducked and flinched away from the light, but Alpha 5 spun excitedly and faced a spot on the wall. When nothing terrible happened, all of the kids looked, too.

Part of the wall came to life, rippling in three dimensions like a holographic version of one of those pin-board toys you could push your hand into and see a raised shape on the other side. The shape became a huge human face surrounded by a bright light. He looked closely at Alpha 5 and spoke in an unknown language. Alpha 5 answered. As the conversation went on, the robot said "Zordon" several times. Was that the holographic man's name?

They got off the platforms and clustered together, scooting away. It still hadn't noticed them.

Jason waved for them all to follow him, and they started sneaking toward the door. Suddenly, Zordon shouted in the alien language, and the door closed in their faces.

"Come forward, please," Alpha 5 said. He added

something else to Zordon in the alien language.

"Do we have a choice?" asked Kimberly.

"I don't think so," Jason replied.

As they moved closer, Alpha 5 turned to them. "Look, it's Zordon."

Sensing their confusion, Alpha 5 turned back to the hologram. "Zordon, I don't think they know who you are."

Zordon looked them over.

"These are them," he said. "They are so small."

Alpha 5 replied, "Funny, I said the same thing, actually."

"You mean to tell me that the fate of the universe has been placed in the hands of these . . . children?"

"They're teenagers," Alpha 5 corrected him. "Somewhere between infancy and full maturity. Very hard to explain, really."

"Show me the coins," Zordon said. They did. He looked at them all and said, "The Morphin Grid is never wrong. If the Power coins returned to the ship with these . . ."

"Teenagers," Alpha 5 prompted.

"Then these *teenagers* are . . . the Power Rangers."

"The Power Rangers!" Alpha 5 exclaimed.

"Quick question," Zack said, half raising one hand. "Hello. Hate to interrupt, but did I just hear you say that we are 'Power Rangers'?"

"Yes," Zordon said. "You are the Power Rangers. Any other questions?"

Zack held his blank expression. "No, I think I'm good."

"Good," Zordon replied.

Billy was practically vibrating with excitement. "I'm Billy, weird Billy Cranston, and . . . well, um, kids used to call me—"

"Billy!" Jason said. They locked eyes.

Billy slowed his breathing. He pointed at the pulsating energy sphere. Images flowed through it. They showed some kind of battle. People trying to get . . . What was that? Some kind of Crystal? "The images here, in this sphere . . . tell a history, and it looks like the Power Rangers are a team that protects life." Billy looked puzzled. "But life is a bright piece of light?"

"Yes, yes! Very good, Billy. It's called the Zeo Crystal," Zordon said.

Alpha 5 perked up. "Oh, I love this part! This is good!"

"And every planet in the universe that has life has a piece of the Crystal buried inside it," Zordon continued.

"Sixty-five million years ago," Alpha 5 added, "Zordon's team died defending the Crystal here in what is now Angel Grove."

"The coins have chosen you five," said Zordon.

"You five!" exclaimed Alpha 5.

"Now you must protect the Zeo Crystal and life on Earth!"

"Because we are the Power Rangers?" Jason asked.

"They're small and stupid," Alpha 5 said.

There was a brief silence. Then Kimberly started to laugh. She tried to control it, but she couldn't, and soon enough all five of them were cracking up.

"I'm sorry," Kimberly said, "but . . . is this a joke?" She waved an arm around at all of them. "I'm standing here with a wet wedgie, my socks are soaked . . . we're talking to the wall . . . I mean, seriously . . ." She started laughing again.

Zordon let her go on for a while, but then the light surrounding his image grew so bright, it nearly blinded them. The low background hum of the ship got louder, too. "SILENCE!" Zordon thundered.

An invisible force picked up all five of the teenagers and held them in midair, flat on their backs. Jason felt himself falling . . .

CHAPTER FOURTEEN

And a moment later, he sat up on the couch in the living room of his house. Everything seemed normal. An after-school cartoon played on the TV. He must have fallen asleep . . . Man, what a dream. Jason went to the front door and opened it—and somehow found himself standing on Main Street in downtown Angel Grove.

Everything was dead. People seemed to have turned into dust statues. Buildings looked like a sneeze would knock them over. Jason stopped and looked around. He saw only one other person.

She was wearing some kind of green costume, walking down the middle of Main Street with a gold staff that rang on the pavement with each step. Jason thought she was beautiful, but scary. Time slipped and she was suddenly right in front of him, smiling in a way that made his stomach flip.

She reached up like she was going to stroke his cheek. He stepped back as her hand made contact, knocking over some of the ash people. They disintegrated as he felt his life drain . . .

Jason snapped back to awareness. He and the rest of the group thumped to the floor as Zordon let them go. "Sir, I'm detecting elevated heart rates," Alpha 5 said. "They're scared."

Jason sat up, angry and frightened. "I don't understand. Why would you show us this nightmare?"

Zordon met his gaze and didn't blink. "It's not a nightmare. It's the future."

"Was it for real?" Kimberly asked.

"It felt like it," Trini replied.

"Who was that woman?"

"Her name is Rita Repulsa. She will create Goldar, a huge monster who will rip the Crystal from the Earth, and all life on your planet will die. With the Crystal, Rita will have the power to create and destroy worlds."

The kids digested this for a moment. Looking at their faces, Jason could tell they'd all had a similar vision, or nightmare, or whatever. They'd all seen this Rita Repulsa.

"So, let me guess," Trini said. "You want us to kill this evil woman? Rita?"

"She must be stopped," Zordon answered.

"When is she coming?" Kimberly asked.

"She's already here!" Alpha 5 replied. "My best guess is we have eleven months. I'm sorry—days! Days. Eleven days."

"If we're Power Rangers, and this is our ship," Trini said. "If I walk to that door, will it open for me?"

"Of course," Zordon said.

She headed for the door. Zack was right on her heels. Billy and Kimberly followed. Jason paused and looked at Zordon.

"Jason, my Ranger team died defending the Crystal from Rita," Zordon said. "It's why I'm in this wall."

Jason started to fire back another sarcastic reply, but . . . "How'd you know my name?"

"It's you, Jason Scott," Zordon said. "You're the Red Ranger. You're the leader."

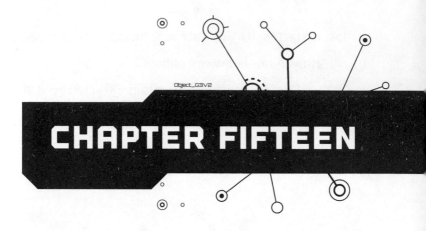

CHAPTER FIFTEEN

In the Morphin Grid, a hologram of the Red Ranger appeared. Jason knew it was crazy, but something about Zordon's story was getting to him. Destiny. Maybe he could be more than a high-school quarterback with a blown-out knee. Maybe . . .

Zordon continued the story as the sphere showed a Green Ranger. "She was a Ranger, too. She was on my team. We were close, but she grew restless . . ." Jason recognized her: an uncorrupted version of the woman in the nightmare. He could tell from Zordon's voice that there was more to the story, but all Zordon said was, "She lost her way. She's now pure evil.

"You must bring them back, all of the Rangers. You

must train your team to stop her before she has enough strength to find the Crystal."

Jason put up his hands. "Okay, I'm leaving and I only speak for myself when I say—"

"NO!" Zordon was in thunder mode again. "YOU SPEAK FOR ALL OF THEM!" Jason stayed put. "You need to lead this team," Zordon went on, more quietly. "You know deep down that what I'm saying is true. You were born for this."

"Sure," Jason said. "Got it. Good night." He started to walk away. Coin or no coin, he was out of there.

"EVERYTHING AND EVERYONE YOU'VE EVER KNOWN WILL DIE!" Zordon boomed.

Jason was surprised to find that the rest of the group was waiting for him when he came back out into the cave. "You all waited. Even you," he added, to whatshername with the tough-girl act. "Who exactly are you?"

"Really? Now you're gonna ask me who I am?"

"Her name's Dede," Zack said.

"Trini," she corrected him.

"She's new at school," Kimberly said. "Transferred in a month ago. We have English together."

"I've been at Angel Grove for over a year. We have *biology* together. Good talk."

She started to walk off, but Jason called after her. "Wait. Look, none of us really know one another. But somehow we were all in the same place, at the same time, when Billy found the coins."

"Wait, wait, wait! Can I ask a question? Are we really like superheroes?" Billy asked. He was getting excited again. "Are we more like Iron Man or Spider-Man? I kinda felt like I got bit by a spider, but I mean, I feel really good."

"Trust me, you're not a superhero, bro," Zack said.

Trini gave Jason some serious side-eye. "Why are you talking to us like you're the boss?"

Kimberly had a different question. "Wait, hold up. Can any of this Rita stuff be real? Can any of it be true?"

"I don't know," Jason replied. "But I know the answer to what's wrong with us, and what's happening to us, is here."

"What are you saying?" Now Kimberly was giving him side-eye, too.

"I think we gotta come back," Jason said. "I can't make you come back here. But, four o'clock tomorrow, I'll be here."

That was all he had to say. He headed back toward the shimmery water–ceilinged cave.

Rita found her way to a group of people standing around a fire in a barrel. No one would look for her here. She set her prizes on top of another barrel: a wedding band, a bracelet, and three gold teeth. Then a gold coin that looked much like a Power Ranger's Power coin. One of the men came up to her. "What are you doing?"

"I need gold. I need to build my beautiful Goldar, dig up the Zeo Crystal, and rule the universe," Rita said.

The man smiled. "Me too!" he said. Rita did not know if he was serious, and did not care. She was entirely focused on the row of gold front teeth exposed by his smile.

She smiled back.

CHAPTER SIXTEEN

Zack wasn't sure about any of this, but he rolled with it. Moving right along. He had things to do. He got all of his mother's pills along with her morning glass of juice and carried a tray into her bedroom. She didn't look great, but she was sick enough that every day, Zack was just glad when she woke up. "You came in so late last night," she said.

Sometimes Zack got frustrated that she would only speak to him in Mandarin at home, but now that she was so sick it didn't bother him anymore. Plus, it kept him in practice.

"Relax, Mom," Zack said. "Just sit up a little bit, okay?" He set the tray on her lap.

"I was happy just to know you'd come home. You're going to school, right? Sometimes?" Zack kissed her on the forehead and headed out of the room. "Zack?! You didn't answer me," she called after him.

"Make sure you take your pills," he replied.

Trini's twin brothers were talking about their basketball game when she came into the kitchen. They got quiet when she came in. "Where were you yesterday?" her mother asked. "Were you with friends? Do you have any friends?"

"This is the problem," her dad said. "You ask her four questions before she's answered the first."

"Well, she's like a ghost around here. She needs to start communicating. Say something. Anything! Speak!" It was quiet for a minute after that.

Then her dad said, "Trini, let's start over. Good morning. Please tell me *one* thing you did yesterday."

Trini looked up from her phone. "Me and four kids from Angel Grove found a spaceship buried underground."

"What?" Her mother sounded equal parts angry and surprised.

Trini nodded, playing it cool. "I'm pretty sure I'm a superhero."

Her mother stormed out of the kitchen. The twins just stared at her. "Cool," they said together.

"Eat your pancakes," their father said to them.

Trini's mother came back with a plastic cup. "Pee in that cup!" she demanded.

You wanted the truth, Trini thought. *Well, you got it.*

Almost late to school, Jason headed out the door in a big rush . . . and stopped dead when he saw his busted-up truck in the driveway. He walked up to it and ran his fingers over the dented metal of the cab. He looked up and saw his father there. "This to remind me of my screwup?"

"No. The junkyard only offered me three hundred bucks for it." His dad looked away. "I figured I'd leave it up to you to decide if you wanted to fix it." He looked back at Jason and smiled. Jason smiled back. Maybe things were going to be okay between them.

A police cruiser pulled up to the end of the driveway, and Sam walked down to meet Captain Bowen. Jason heard part of the conversation. They spoke about one of his dad's deckhands. The news wasn't good. *If I'd been there,* Jason thought, *I would have defended them. I would have helped.*

At four o'clock, they were all there outside the mine entrance. Together, they went back inside the spaceship and met Zordon in the control room. "You need to follow the three rules to being a Power Ranger. You must never use your powers for personal gain," Zordon said. "You must never escalate a fight unless your enemy forces you to. And you must never reveal your identity. Ever."

The kids exchanged looks. This Zordon guy was serious.

"To assume your Ranger identity, you must morph," he went on. "You all have morphed before, haven't you?"

None of them were sure what he meant.

"Step into the footprints, please," Alpha 5 said. "Let's try this."

One by one, they did. When they were all in place, Zordon said, "Standing in this circle, as a team, you can easily connect to the Morphin Grid. Do you feel it?"

They looked at each other. Zack spoke for all of them when he said, "Nope. Not feeling it."

Zordon ignored his sarcasm. "You need to morph to get your armor. Clear your minds."

"Yes! We get armor!" Billy shouted. "I knew it!"

Zack agreed. "So cool! When do you give us the armor?"

"I don't," Zordon said. "It's already inside of you. You bring it out by connecting to each other and connecting to the Morphin Grid."

For the first time, Zordon smiled. "Clear your minds. Focus."

All five of them stood silently.

"The Power Rangers are a legion of warriors sworn to protect life," Zordon added. "You must become those warriors."

The lights in the Morphin Grid surrounding the sphere got brighter . . . but after an awkward silence, they were all still just standing there.

"Alpha 5, why didn't they morph?" Zordon asked.

"I don't know." Alpha 5 ran around looking at the grid. "Disturbing. This may take some time. Zordon, if they can't morph, what are we supposed to do?" Alpha 5 added.

Zordon thought this over for a moment. "They'll have to train without armor. They need to prepare."

"Without armor?" Alpha 5 looked to Zordon. "Sir, that will be very painful."

"Take them to the Pit," Zordon commanded.

"Oh, brother," Alpha 5 replied, then, to the others, "All right, follow me. We're going down to the Pit!"

CHAPTER SEVENTEEN

The Pit? Jason didn't like the sound of that. But they'd come too far to back out now. Alpha 5 led them into the big open space under the ship. "This is the Pit! Nice, right?"

Zordon's voice echoed around them. "I invite you all to stand in the Pit, please. Alpha 5, begin the exercise." Zordon sounded irritated.

"All right, good luck!" Alpha 5 stretched out one arm about twenty feet to the underside of the ship. Lights flashed and rippled as three large rock creatures emerged from the cave floor.

Alpha 5 peered at one of the creatures. "This one looks

like Norman." Then he looked to one of the other ones. "But it's not Norman because this one is Norman. Hey, Norman!"

"These creatures before you are a simulation of Rita's army," said Zordon. "They're called putties. You must get through them to get to her."

All of the kids dropped into fighting crouches. Not all of them knew how to fight, but they were going to try.

"Relax," Zack said. "It's just a hologram. It's like a video game!"

The creature backhanded Zack across the Pit. He crashed into a heap.

"That's a strong hologram," said Billy.

Zack nodded in agreement. "Not a video game."

"This is why you must morph into your armor," Zordon added. "If Rita becomes strong enough to build them, it could be the beginning of the end. Rangers, welcome to training."

More of them appeared. Jason couldn't tell how many, but suddenly they were everywhere. Jason went after them, trying to help his teammates who weren't good fighters. Billy went down. Then Kimberly. Jason was holding his own against a pair of the creatures, but another one hit him from behind and his legs went out from under him.

Trini was a revelation, the last one standing and completely calm as she punched and spun and kicked. Jason's head started to clear. She inspired him to get back in the fight . . . but right as he got up, all of the creatures disappeared. Alpha 5 had stopped the exercise.

"Rita uses anything in her environment to make creatures to fight for her," Alpha 5 explained.

"She can make these things whenever she wants?" Trini asked. "How do you expect us to stop her?"

"Like all of you, she has a coin," Zordon said. "She's connected to the Morphin Grid and she knows how to gain power from it."

"If we can catch her before she is at full strength, we have a chance," Alpha 5 added.

Zordon's tone grew somber. "But you must morph first. Or you will die."

"The news just keeps getting better," Kimberly remarked.

CHAPTER EIGHTEEN

The five would-be Power Rangers were together in the Pit and once again surrounded by putties.

"Aim for the center mass!" Alpha 5 called out. "Slip the punch! Find their weak side!"

Zack went for the closest putty, but was easily knocked back.

"You need to learn the element of surprise!" Alpha 5 added.

The Rangers struggled to work as a team, each one fighting as an individual—and failing.

"Your team's journey of a thousand miles begins with

the first step," Zordon called out. "Together. You have to connect to each other. You must shed your masks to wear this armor. Alpha 5, restart the exercise—"

"Wait!" Jason said. "Just wait." He turned from Alpha 5 to the rest of the kids. "Let's figure out a way to fight together. I know martial arts, and, Trini? You kicked butt last time."

"When you're the new girl, you need to know how to fight," she said.

Jason nodded. "You heard what Zordon said . . . let's teach each other what we know."

And they did. By the end of their third day together, they were doing better. The putties were still winning, but it was more of a fight. The next day, Alpha 5 started fooling around with someone's phone. "I've made an amazing discovery!" he said with delight. "Music!" After that, they trained to a sound track. Everything from classical to hip-hop.

By the end of the fourth day, they were making progress. Even Jason and Zack seemed to have pulled together. In detention that next Saturday, Kimberly,

Jason, and Billy didn't sit together, but they could feel a connection. On Sunday, Kimberly and Trini went to a coffee shop. They were starting to be friends, and it was good to get away from the boys. Zordon was worried that none of them had morphed yet. Kimberly was worried about the news from around town. Fires, weird crimes . . .

CHAPTER NINETEEN

Billy spent a lot of time with a notebook, staring at the weird images in the Morphin Grid and writing things down, determined to learn the location of the Crystal.

"Hey, Billy," Alpha 5 called to him. "I know we're trying to find the Crystal and everything . . . but . . . uh, the other guys like me, right?" Billy just looked at him, not sure how to respond. "You think Zordon likes me?" he added.

Billy still didn't say anything.

"Do you think I'm smart?" Alpha 5 asked. "Billy . . . you listening?"

As a group, they still hadn't morphed. They were getting better at fighting, at least.

"Think only of each other," Zordon instructed, "and the Morphin Grid will open to you." The Rangers looked at each other, not sure what to do.

"If Rita manages to create Goldar and he rips the Crystal from the ground," Alpha 5 said, "it'll be like ten thousand nuclear bombs washing over Earth."

"You bring this up now?" Zack said. "Is this supposed to freak us out?"

"It's working," Billy said.

"You keep making this harder," Jason said. "We're busting our butts. Feel free to throw us a bone at some point."

"Yes, yes," Alpha 5 said. "I see you busting your butts. So I've decided to give you some inspiration." He led them to a rock wall on their way down to the Pit. When they reached it, he gestured toward the top. "What you will find beyond this wall will forever change your lives."

They scaled the wall, and as the kids got a look at what lay to the other side, Alpha 5 added, "The Zords! Pretty cool, right?"

In the cave beyond the wall stood five huge animal-like machines, keyed to the colors of each Ranger's coin. A red Tyrannosaurus rex, a blue triceratops, a pink pterodactyl, a black mastodon, a yellow saber-toothed tiger. Like it was Christmas morning, the kids ran among the huge machines, each finding the one that matched their coin. *Who needs armor,* Jason thought, *when you can jump into a sixty-foot mechanical T. rex with some kind of laser guns instead of arms? Wow.*

"Zords take on the forms of the most powerful organisms on the planet," Alpha 5 called out, his voice echoing in the huge space. "When these Zords formed, dinosaurs reigned supreme. They will be an extension of you, and their power will be all but limitless! But you're not ready yet for this power! Let's go train. Today's the day, Rangers. I feel it!"

They were inspired to hit the Pit after seeing the Zords. But when they got there . . .

"Where's Zack?" Alpha 5 asked.

No way was Zack going to see something like his freaking awesome huge black eight-legged mastodon Zord and not take it for a spin. Training, schmaining. He was Zording! Only problem was, he hadn't really figured out how to do it. The minute he got into the cockpit, up in the mastodon's head, it went charging off—through the side of the mountain. Blasting through into daylight, it raced out across the open ground. "Aaaaahhhhh!" Zack was yelling. He tried to get it under control—and did, just before it almost broadsided a church van zooming down the highway. Inside the van, Zack saw the faces of astonished nuns. He waved. He was finally getting a handle on how to drive his Zord!

But he realized he'd better get out of there. People would notice. He turned it around and rumbled back toward the hole he'd made in the mountain.

By the time he got there, he was hotdogging a little, and when he tried to slow down, he wiped out. The Zord plowed into the ground, showering the rest of the Rangers with rocks. He popped the cockpit canopy and jumped out. "My bad! That's on me, right there."

Just as his feet touched the ground, Trini was on him. "What's your problem?" she shouted, poking him in the chest. Then Jason had him by the arm.

"You could have killed yourself!" Jason snapped. "Or us!"

Zack shoved him away. "Back off, boss man!"

Jason stepped back up to him—and the fight was on. They grappled to the ground, both landing punches. Trini tried to wedge herself between them as Kimberly tried to pull everyone apart. Only Billy hung back. He was trying to work himself up to join, but he didn't know what to do . . .

Finally, he jumped right into the middle of all four of them. "Stop!" he shouted at the top of his lungs. "You'll kill each other!"

"That's enough!" Zordon bellowed. "When will you learn to act like Rangers? Training is over for today. Go home. All of you."

No, Jason thought. *That's not how this goes.* He cut through the circle and followed Alpha 5 into the ship.

Object_G3V2

CHAPTER TWENTY

He could hear Zordon ranting before he got to the control room. "Jason's team is failing. I will destroy Rita myself. There must be a way to free me from this wall!"

Alpha 5 stayed patient. "Yes, but the irony is you need these Rangers to morph! If they morph, you can harness that energy to regenerate your body and come back through!"

"There has to be another way," Zordon growled. "I can't—"

Jason had heard enough. He stepped into the control room. "You can't *what*?" he asked defiantly. "Wait for us dumb kids to morph so that you can come back?" He waited for them to deny it. "That's what all this has been about, right? You coming back?"

"This has only ever been about protecting the Crystal!" Zordon boomed. "Rita could be building Goldar as we speak!"

"Don't underestimate me or my team," said Jason.

"You can't stop him," Zordon added. "She will have him dig up the Crystal, and life on Earth will die."

"And we need you because you were so successful at stopping her last time?" Jason shot back.

"I died burying those coins in the hopes that they would find the next real Rangers!" Zordon raged. "Those who are worthy!"

"Sorry to disappoint you! And I don't need to stand here and have you tell me what I did wrong. I can go home and get that."

"Jason, you need me out of this wall. To help lead this team!"

"Your team is dead," Jason said. "And you're just as scared as we are."

Then he left to catch up with the rest of the Rangers.

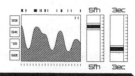

CHAPTER
TWENTY-ONE

Drawn by her sense that gold was near, Rita Repulsa walked into a jewelry store and slapped down a hand on the glass counter. In her other hand, she held her staff. "I'm interested in gold," she said. Water trickled from her hand onto the countertop. "All of your gold." Rita held up the staff. All of the charms and bracelets and teeth were worked into it. Soon, she would be able to use its full power.

The store worker bent behind the case and quickly pushed the panic button. She stood up and started putting trays of gold jewelry on the counter. Rita picked up a handful of the gold and placed it in her mouth. She smiled. She grabbed the rest and began molding it onto her staff. She pulled the terrified store worker to her, checking the woman's teeth for gold. Noticing her gold necklace, Rita hissed, "Give it to me!"

Rita snapped off the necklace and pressed it into her staff.

The staff was almost finished. Rita drew out her coin, the precious coin that held her connection to the Morphin Grid. It would go in a circular hole near the head of the staff, and then her true powers would begin to show.

The front door chimed and someone shouted, "Police! Don't move! Drop your . . . weapon and put your hands on your head! Do it now! Do what I say, lady!"

Rita turned to see a person in some kind of uniform pointing a weapon at her. "'Lady' . . . I like the sound of 'lady.'"

"Get on the ground and you won't get hurt," yelled the officer.

Instead, she brought her hands together to put the coin in the hole.

A loud boom sounded as he fired his shotgun at her. Rita felt a heavy punch right below her sternum. The impact knocked her sprawling backward over the glass counter.

The customers screamed as Rita sat up. "I have a headache," she announced. She placed the coin in the hole at the head of her staff. It began to glow, and the entire store began to vibrate with new energy.

The man fired again, but the weapon had no effect on her. "It's been so long," she said. "Too long . . . since I've raised my beautiful creatures . . ." Glass shattered and metal bent as a putty began to emerge from the floor and the broken jewelry cases. Rita smiled at it. "Did you miss me?" she asked. Then she left as a fire began to spread inside the building. The putty was having its fun.

While the other four waited for Jason to come out of the cave, they debated what to do.

"Hey," Zack said. "Listen, I was gonna stay up here tonight. Make a fire. I have some food if you guys want to stay."

They all started setting down their gear near a high ledge. As the sun went down, they built a fire and dug into the bag of Zack's food. "Look at all this junk," Trini said. "What would Zordon say?"

Imitating Zordon, Zack cracked them all up. "If I wasn't in this wall, I would eat that junk food!"

Billy seemed to know there was more to it than that. "What happened back there?"

"Nothing. Don't worry about it." After a pause, Jason asked them all a question. "What are you guys thinking about when we're trying to morph?"

"I don't know," Billy replied.

They looked at Jason and realized what he was doing. Kimberly did her own Zordon imitation. "You must shed your masks to wear this armor."

Billy was next. "Think only of each other and the Morphin Grid will open for you!"

"Maybe we don't know each other," Zack said more soberly. "And that's why we can't morph." The rest looked at him, surprised he was being so candid. "I'm serious. You don't know me." He laughed and stood up. "Let's do this for real. I'm Zack and I'm a Power Ranger."

They all laughed. "Hi, Zack . . ."

"Truth," he went on. "I live in the Melody Mobile Home Park. It's just me and my mom. And my mom is the best. But my mom . . . she's sick right now, so she can't work. I do what I can, but I'm scared. Sometimes I'm too scared to stay there at night, because I'm afraid she's not gonna make it. And if she goes, when she goes . . . I got no one else. I think being with you guys is good for me." He sat back down.

"Let's do that. Let's tell our secrets," Billy said. "It'll help us. Okay, I got a secret." They all waited. "I like country music. As a matter of fact, I love country music." Over the laughter that followed, he kept talking. "And I don't miss my dad. As much. Coming to the mine with him was all I had. But coming here with you guys is just as good."

They all felt that, Jason thought. "Bigger secret is why were you in detention?" he prompted Billy.

"I blew up my lunch box. Accident. It was an accident! My lunchbox was in my locker. Boom goes the dynamite, into detention goes Billy!" Everyone laughed. Billy pointed across the fire. "Let's not forget that Kimberly Hart was in detention, too!"

"That's right," Trini added.

They all looked at Kimberly. She looked down. "No," she said. "Not tonight. Skip me."

"What about you?" Billy asked Jason. "Want to tell us who you really are?"

"Everyone knows exactly who I am," Jason said, trying to brush off the question.

"What about the crazy girl?" Zack asked, trying to get a rise out of Trini.

"I could tell you anything, and you'd never know if it was true or not," Trini said with a laugh. Then she got serious. "Okay. I'm the new girl. Always. Three schools in three years. What's crazy is that I like it that way. It's just easier. Nobody ever has to get to know me, and my parents don't have to worry about my relationships."

"Boyfriend troubles?" asked Zack.

"Yeah," Trini replied with a sneer. "Boyfriend troubles."

Zack gave her a quizzical look.

"My family is so normal. Too normal," she added. "They believe in labels. They'd like for me to dress differently, talk more, have the kind of friends they want me to have. I don't know how to tell them what's really going on with me." She paused and looked at the rest of them, watching them watching her. "I've never said any of this out loud."

"It's cool. You're with us now," Billy said. He held out a fist but she left him hanging.

"Am I? What does that mean? When this is all over . . . are we Power Rangers or are we friends?"

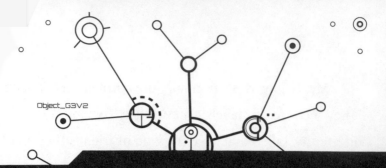
CHAPTER TWENTY-TWO

Trini decided to go home. After opening up to the rest of the Rangers, she needed some alone time. She climbed through her bedroom window and just let her mind wander. An hour later, she was sound asleep.

She woke up to the sensation of water dripping on her face. Rain? A leak? What could it—?

That woman was floating above her. Rita Repulsa. A soft green glow surrounded her and her staff. She was beautiful and evil and terrifying all at once. "Do you know who I am?" she asked quietly. Trini nodded. "I was once just like you. So pretty. Innocent. Say my name."

"Rita . . . Repulsa," Trini replied in a trembling voice.

Then Trini got angry. She grabbed Rita, but Rita spun her around and pinned her to the ceiling.

"Delightful," she said. "Have you morphed yet?" She slammed Trini into the wall. Trini tried not to show her fear. "That was a trick question," Rita said. She smelled like the bottom of the ocean, cold and salty and dead. "If you could morph, we'd be having a very different conversation. The Yellow Ranger. Should I kill you?" She leaned close and whispered in Trini's ear. "Oh, you want your armor! I'll show you mine if you show me yours."

Rita's armor started to push out through her skin. It was charred and spiky, corrupted. But Trini could see that once it had been like a Green Ranger's armor. Trini grabbed her again, trying to get her in a choke hold. Rita struggled. "Please no, you're hurting me! You're so strong!" Then she relaxed and smiled. "Just kidding."

Rita broke Trini's grip and pinned her against the wall. "You have spunk, little Yellow," she said, leaning close. "I see myself in you. And in your heart, you know it. Come with me. We can be friends." She moved back enough for Trini to feel like she could breathe again. "All I need to know is . . . where is the Zeo Crystal?"

"I don't know," Trini said.

Rita studied her. "Sadly, I believe you. Tomorrow, I am going to destroy Angel Grove. But in exchange for your life . . . you will find out where the Crystal is and you will come to me. We can have a deal, Dede my friend."

CHAPTER
TWENTY-THREE

Jason snapped awake late that night and found Kimberly sitting on the side of his bed. "How did you get in here?"

"I'm a superhero," she said. "And you left your window open."

He sat up and quickly checked the hallway before shutting his door.

"I'm the reason we can't morph. I haven't been honest," she said.

Jason started to say something, but Kimberly held up a hand. "Listen to me," she said, "I punched Ty Fleming in the face because he told everyone I was the meanest person he'd ever met. And he was right."

"That can't be true."

Kimberly scrolled through her phone's pictures and held one up for him to see. Jason grimaced and looked away. "Whoa. You took that picture?"

"No," Kimberly said. "Amanda took that picture of herself. But she shared it with me, privately. She trusted me."

"You sent that pic to Ty?"

She nodded.

"And he sent it to . . . someone who sent it to someone . . . ," Jason added.

"Until it got back to her," Kimberly finished. "I didn't realize how mean it was until I saw her face."

"Kim, there's literally thousands of photos going around school."

"I don't care about them. I care about this. I had to sit in Mr. Detmer's office with Amanda's father and watch as they showed him that photo of his daughter. He's known me my whole life. Like, I literally grew up in his house. He looked at that picture, and for the first time, in his eyes, I could see who I'd become." She was trying not to cry.

"So I lied. I blamed everyone else for it. I wanted to die."

"Okay, listen. Start over. Erase that picture, right now," Jason said.

"Jason. It can't be erased."

"Then live with it. You did an awful thing. It doesn't make you an awful person."

"Okay. Any more wisdom for me?"

"Just . . . " He paused. "Be the person you want to be."

"Honestly," she said, "I kind of want to be the girl who kisses you right now, Cheesy, right?"

This caught Jason off guard. "Well . . . yeah . . . so . . . um . . . I think you should be that girl. But it's up to you."

CHAPTER
TWENTY-FOUR

Just after four in the morning, Jason, Billy, Kimberly, and Zack arrived at the football field.

"We all got the same text," Kimberly said. "So where is she?"

Had Trini joined Rita? Had she sent them the message to draw them out? They were sitting ducks out there in the middle of the field.

Then they heard Trini's voice. "I'm here." She joined the circle, obviously shaken and scared.

They all stood in silence before she finally spoke.

"Look, Rita came to my house tonight," Trini said. Now they could all see the cuts and bruises on her face.

"Yeah, she's real. Insane. She nearly killed me." Trini paused, looking at the cuts on her wrists. "She was trying to get me to join her. She said she'd spare my life if I could keep a secret."

"What secret?" Zack asked.

"At dawn, this morning, the destruction of Angel Grove begins."

"This is real," Kimberly added. "This is the end."

"No. It's not," Jason replied.

There was already a faint hint of light in the east. "Where is she?" he asked.

"She said to meet her where the dead ships live," Trini said.

"Okay. That's the salvage yard by the docks," Jason said. "Let's go."

No one moved.

Jason was shocked. "Are you serious? No one?"

"Jason, we're not even Power Rangers yet," Trini said.

"I say we go back to Zordon," Billy added.

It's time for them to hear the truth, Jason thought. "Zordon thinks we're a joke. He said it to my face."

Visibly upset, Billy asked, "So this was all a lie?"

"Of course it was a lie, Billy!" He saw he was upsetting them and he didn't care. "What, am I hurting your feelings? Grow up. We failed. Let's stop being delusional about being a team of superheroes."

"*We* are," Billy said, emphasizing *we*. He pointed to everyone in the group but Jason. "We are a team!"

"We are?" Jason snapped. "We don't even know each other."

"No," Billy fired back. "The only person in this circle we don't know is *you*."

Whoa, Jason thought. *Billy Cranston draws blood.* "You wanna know me? Fine. You think that's gonna change anything?" He laughed, solely out of frustration. "You wanna know the deep, dark secret about Jason Scott? People expect me to do great things." He adopted his father's voice. *"C'mon, Jay! Get it done. It's on you now! It's all you, you got this!"* Then he was himself again. "I'm so tired of being what everyone else wants me to be! So I burned it all down. One crazy stunt after the next. When those cops were chasing me, I knew it was all over. I flipped that truck, crushed my knee. The pain was insane, but all I felt was relief." He hadn't meant to reveal so much, but now that he had, Jason saw he was speaking to friends. Then he added, "I'm tired, okay? I'm tired. And as much as I hate this scrubby town, I don't want to just sit around and watch it die, okay? We are all screwups. But can we at least go and do the one thing that's been asked of us and kill Rita?"

With a smile at Jason, Kimberly said, "You know this is a bad idea, right?"

"The worst," he said. "Let's vote. Show of hands."

Five hands rose in the darkness.

CHAPTER TWENTY-FIVE

They got to the salvage yard while it was still dark, scaling and leaping over boats toward a large open building in the middle of the yard. A barrel fire burned inside, and a figure slumped in a chair near the barrel.

They went inside, looking past the barrel to the docks and the harbor beyond. There was music playing. When they got closer, they saw that the figure was a homeless man. He was bound and gagged. The music came from a boom box hung around his neck. He looked terrified. Trini got closer to him, seeing he was trying to tell her something with his eyes.

A drop of water landed on his cheek. Then another.

Another landed on Trini's palm, and she figured it out. "Oh no," she said, and looked up.

There was a little more light in the sky when they came to their senses, but it wasn't yet dawn. They hung over the side of a boat docked at the edge of the salvage yard, tangled in ropes and nets at Rita's eye level.

"Five little Rangers, tied up like fish," she hissed as she stepped in front of Jason. "The leader? Hello, Red."

Jason slammed his head into Rita's. She drew back slightly and gave him a sly look.

"You're not entirely disappointing," she said, her eyes fixed on his. "Oh, look at you, trying to figure out my plan. I'll just tell you! Yellow has led you to your deaths, 'cause I'm going to kill you one by one until you tell me—where's my Crystal?"

"We don't know," Jason said.

"No, Red. You don't know. But guess what? One of you does!" She walked along the line of Rangers. "Who could it be? Pink? I bet if I gave you one guess, you'd get it right. Eeny meeny miny . . ." She stopped in front of

Billy, moved on . . . and then came back. "Blue. So loyal. So pure of heart," she said.

Billy tried to hide it, but he couldn't. He'd seen the clues in the Morphin Grid and he'd figured it out. But he couldn't tell her.

"Tell the class what you know! Just tell us, Blue. Where's my Crystal?" Billy kept his mouth shut. "You can tell me now, Blue—or you can tell me after I kill all of your friends," Rita said. "Let's start with Black?"

She touched the tip of her staff to Zack's throat. He started to choke. "He dies in three . . . two—"

"Okay! Don't hurt my friends, all right?" Billy called out.

Rita moved her staff, and Zack heaved a huge breath.

Billy looked at Jason, who nodded. "It's under . . . a dining establishment," Billy said.

"Where? What does that mean?" Rita hissed. "What's it called?"

"It's a Krispy Kreme!"

"Krispy Kreme. This is a special place!"

"Very special," Billy added.

"Must be," she said to herself. "The source of life itself is buried there. Thank you, Blue," Rita said. "For being so weak." She paused, then made a decision. "Zordon would lose all respect for me if I didn't kill you. At least one of you."

She waved her staff and Billy, still trapped in the net, dropped into the water. The rope holding the net unspooled, then grew taut. It thrashed for a while . . . and then it was still.

"As a reward for your valor," Rita said. "Now watch your town die."

She swung her staff again, and the rest of the kids fell. As soon as they got themselves free, they started hauling Billy back up.

"He's going to be okay, right?" Trini asked.

Jason tried to comfort her, but Kimberly interrupted. "He's dead."

They looked at each other, stunned and unsure what to do next.

Rita walked away, her work done for the moment.

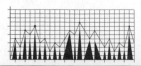

CHAPTER
TWENTY-SIX

It was just after dawn when they carried Billy's body into the control room.

Alpha 5 zoomed out to meet them, and Zordon's face appeared in the wall, his expression grave.

"Do something, okay?" Jason said. "There must be something you can do for him."

"I told you that you are not ready," Zordon replied.

"Zordon," he pleaded. "Please help us. Okay? Please."

Zordon was sad but firm. "There's nothing I can do for him. We were both reckless with our teams."

"I'm sorry," Jason said softly as he turned and walked back over to Billy. *Of all of us*, he thought, *Billy was the*

best. The kindest, the smartest . . . "I'm sorry, guys. He's dead because of me."

Kimberly shook her head. "No, Jason, it was all of us."

"I pushed it," Jason went on. "And, as usual, I made the wrong decision, out of fear . . . anger. I was just so angry. He's a great kid, you know? He loved us. He loved being a Ranger." The light in the Morphin Grid was getting brighter, just like it had the first time they stepped into it. "I'm sorry, Billy. I'd trade my life for yours if I could."

Kimberly stood next to him. "Maybe he traded his life for us."

"He probably did," Zack said. He looked at the rest of them, one after another. "I would."

"Me too," Kimberly said.

Softly, Trini said it, too.

"It's just the four of us now," Kimberly said. The Morphin Grid blazed. "The truth is, whatever we've said to each other . . . it doesn't matter. This? This is the only thing that matters."

"She's right," Trini added.

At the edge of the room, Alpha 5 sidled up to Zordon.

"Look at the grid. This is your time! Do you see it? The grid is open! Step through."

"I see it," Zordon said. His face vanished.

The kids were all still locked in their bonding moment. Intense morphing energy created wind that rocked them on their feet. "What's happening?" Zack shouted over the sound.

"The Morphin Grid is open!" Alpha 5 shouted back.

The sound and light reached a crescendo . . . and slowly faded. "Zordon? Master?" Alpha 5 said into the silence that followed. "He must have stepped through the grid."

Kimberly looked around. "Alpha, where'd he go?"

"I have no idea where he is," Alpha 5 replied.

The wall pixels flickered and Zordon's face appeared. "Why didn't you step through? That was your only chance." Alpha 5 sounded confused. Jason was wondering the same thing.

"I know," Zordon replied. "But only one can come back."

Something moved in the room behind them. They

turned and saw Billy getting to his feet. He looked beat up, exhausted, still dripping wet, confused . . . but alive.

Trini, Kimberly, and Zack soon had Billy wrapped up in a group hug. He was still a bit wobbly on his feet. "Did I die?" he asked.

"No," Kimberly said.

At the same time, Trini said, "Yes."

Billy knew which one of them to believe. "And you brought me back to life? I told you we were superheroes!"

Jason spun back to Zordon, realizing what the old Ranger had done. "There can be only one Red Ranger," Zordon said quietly. "Jason, this is your time. This is your team."

Jason ran over to Billy and gave him a massive hug. "Welcome back, my friend."

Billy's huge grin faded as something else occurred to him. "We've got to go to Krispy Kreme, Jason."

Zack gave him a look. "What?"

"Not for donuts," Billy added.

"Okay, let's try this," said Jason. He then gave Zordon a respectful bow and offered his thanks. He understood the sacrifice Zordon had just made, bringing Billy back to life instead of resurrecting his own body. That was a true leader.

"Come on, guys," Jason said, walking toward the Morphin Grid. They were already right there with him. They stepped into the footprints. Jason felt like he should say something inspiring, but all he could think of was, "It's Morphin' time."

A rising hum vibrated through the ship. Each of the five friends felt the transformation coming. Jason saw his coin, shining and brilliant. The crust was gone, and the strange outline inside it was now clearly a T. rex.

A flare of light from the Morphin Grid washed over all five of them. As it passed, the Power Rangers looked at each other in their full armor, crackling with the energy of the Morphin Grid.

Jason ran one gloved hand over his other forearm, feeling the smooth, solid armor over the flexible underlayer.

They were all masked now, identifiable only by color: Jason's red, Billy's blue, Kimberly's pink, Trini's yellow,

Zack's black. They had done it! But on the other hand, they hadn't really done anything yet. Rita Repulsa was still out there.

As a group, the Rangers charged out of the ship.

CHAPTER TWENTY-SEVEN

Object_T1349

Rita left a little surprise for the would-be Rangers, then made her way to the bottom of an enormous quarry. It cut down through millions of years of rock, which made it perfect for her needs. She had lost Goldar sixty-five million years ago. It was time to bring him back. With her staff held high over her head, she cried out, "Come back to me, Goldar!"

A deep, seismic rumble sounded all through the quarry. Small trickles of gold appeared and ran together into wider streams that began to drip upward, into the air. More gold flowed from the rocks, pouring up into a mass that hovered above Rita's head. Molten gold dripped and rained around Rita as the mass grew and began to take shape. It joined with the gold still flowing out of the ground, forming an immense pair of legs. Then the torso and head formed—and then arms holding brutal twin swords, each longer than a semitruck. Rita looked up and saw Goldar spread his wings and roar. The sound thundered out over the rocks, and Rita laughed with delight. What a creation he was! A hundred feet tall, pure gold, armored and invincible, and devoted only to her.

"I've missed you, my friend," she said.

Goldar threw back his head, roaring again. What Zordon's meteor had blasted apart, Rita's power had remade! Together they turned and began their march on Angel Grove. Rita would find this Krispy Kreme, and then nothing would stop her.

Now was the time. The Zeo Crystal would be hers.

CHAPTER TWENTY-EIGHT

As the Rangers reached the watery-ceilinged cave, they saw a putty, shimmering on the other side of the water. "How did he find us?" Zack wondered. "We gotta crush him."

"Wait," Trini said. A wave of other putties jumped into the water, blocking the way out.

Kimberly tensed. "Let's do this." She sprang up into the water ceiling. The other Rangers were right there with her.

As Jason approached the putties, he felt a change in his armor—an addition. He looked down to see that a sword had morphed at his side. He drew the blade and immediately felt its power.

All the Rangers could do was fight their way through. As one, the team charged into the putties. The water surged and boiled around them as they fought in full armor, tearing the putties apart—but there were always more. They battled on, fighting the putties until they all burst through the surface of the pool and out into the chasm.

The struggle continued on the ledges and slopes of the rocks around the chasm. Putties appeared from everywhere. The Power Rangers broke them to pieces, shattered them into clouds of dust, threw them off ledges. "There's more coming!" Kimberly shouted, just when they thought they might have a break.

"Guys, they just keep coming!" Jason called out.

Billy spun a kick into the head of a putty. Pieces of it splattered the others nearby. "There's too many of them!"

"You guys hold them off," Zack called out as he disengaged from the melee.

Trini turned to see him vanish into the chaos of the battle. "Zack, where are you going?"

She waited for a response, but none came.

Overwhelmed, she returned her focus to the fight. "Don't stop!" Trini called out to the others. They had to stick together to the end.

The putties pressed close, forcing the Power Rangers toward the edge of a cliff. There was nowhere they could go. Then they heard a rumbling noise, from over the nearest hill.

Zack's Zord appeared over the crest of the hill, scattering the putties and driving them over the edge of the cliff. Zack popped out of the cockpit. "You guys gotta get one of these!" he shouted. Even Jason was happy to see that he'd been reckless enough to take a chance.

They were feeling pretty good about themselves until Billy—who was looking across the broken landscape of the mine area—said, "Uh, guys . . . we're too late."

All of the others followed the direction of Billy's gaze, and there they got their first look at Goldar.

"Oh, man," Zack said. "That's a lot of gold."

Trini headed back toward the cave. "We're going to protect the Crystal, right?"

There was a silence. Then Jason said, "Look. You saw what Rita did to us, and now she's got Goldar."

"We are going to Angel Grove," Kimberly said.

"Then let's get the Zords!" added Trini.

Zack was first into his Zord. He gave the rest of them advice while he rode it up to the top of the hill. "After you power up, gently lean forward, and your Zord will follow your lead," he said. "Easy . . . slow at first." Nobody answered. "Guys, is anyone coming up here?"

In a shower of falling rocks, the other four Zords crashed out of the cave. Trini's saber-toothed tiger scampered between the triceratops and T. rex, with Kimberly's pterodactyl swooping overhead. Zack jumped back into his Zord. "Great! You guys are doing great! Try to stay close . . . whoa, not that close!" Billy crashed into him and then steered away. "Kimberly, how you doing?"

The pterodactyl shot straight up in the air. "AHHHHHHHHHH!!!!" Kimberly screamed.

Trini had the tiger all figured out. She loped along, smooth and fierce, singing an old eighties song: "And the last known survivor stalks his prey in the night . . ."

The rest of them sang along as they rumbled toward Angel Grove, the town they said they hated but were going to save anyway.

CHAPTER TWENTY-NINE

Kimberly watched from the air as Rita and Goldar strode down Main Street. Molten gold fell around her like rain. It crackled on the asphalt and started fires in trees that were too close.

"Guys! Our town!" Kimberly called out. "She's destroying it."

Closing in, the Rangers had to be fast and careful at the same time, so they didn't squash any people. Jason stomped on a parked car and stopped to kick it away.

As Kimberly approached, she reported back to the others. "Rita and her golden boy haven't found Krispy Kreme!"

"Kimberly, you hold them there," Jason said. "Zack, Billy, circle the Krispy Kreme and make sure it's safe. I'm heading straight for Goldar!"

"Copy," Kimberly replied. "Going around."

"Kim, I'll go with you," Trini added.

"Let's go," Zack said. "Billy, it's just the two of us." The mastodon and triceratops peeled away. Trini's saber-toothed tiger headed to help Kimberly, who was firing away at Rita with the pterodactyl's wing-mounted guns.

"Surprise!" she sang out.

Rita looked up. "How cute! The Rangers found their costumes and their dino-cars! Let's give them something else to play with." She struck her staff against the street. Putties came to life as she passed, forming from traffic lights and parked cars. Rita called to her creations, "Crush them!"

Billy looked out at the oncoming putties. "How many does she need?"

The putties shambled north to stop the Zords as Rita and Goldar kept going south. "Jason, watch out!" Kimberly called.

"They're already here," Jason said grimly. An army of putties swarmed over the T. rex. "I can't get them off."

"Turn your head," Kimberly called. "Trust me."

Jason pulled the controls, moving the T. rex's head just as Kimberly jetted in his direction. Her pterodactyl blazed past, knocking the putties to the ground.

"Thanks, Kim," Jason replied as he regained control of the fight.

Over to the west, the same thing was happening to Billy and Zack. Billy's triceratops tipped over and crushed a wall of putties.

Energy blasts from the triceratops's horns vaporized huge groups of putties. "Guns?! I have guns!" Billy couldn't believe his good luck.

Zack charged forward to flip the triceratops back on its feet.

Back on Main Street, Trini and Kimberly tag-teamed Goldar, hitting him high and low. They couldn't bring him down. Rita stood on the high school's roof, looking for something . . .

"Rangers!" Kimberly called. "She just found it."

She strafed the putties again but couldn't get to Rita.

"Okay, come on! Let's move!" Jason's T. rex swept a group of putties aside with its tail.

Billy was already moving, his triceratops's six legs churning at top speed. "Zack and I are closest! We'll try to push Goldar toward the water!"

They got to the intersection of Sixth and Main, close to the Krispy Kreme, at the same time as Goldar.

A few blocks away, Jason had finally shed the last of the putties. He headed toward Goldar, picking up speed. When he got close enough, he launched the T. rex into a feetfirst leap, smashing into Goldar, sending him staggering.

"Come on, Rangers, join me!" Jason called out.

Trini pulled her saber-toothed tiger toward Goldar. After seeing Jason's first blow, she momentarily felt that Goldar might be easy to defeat. As she got closer, though, she could sense his power. It wasn't long before both she and Jason were shaken free.

"We gotta do better!" Jason called out to the others.

"I'm coming!" Kimberly replied as the shadow of her

pterodactyl tore across the battlefield.

Jason reared up his T. rex, readying another strike. On the periphery of the destroyed street he saw a familiar truck getting hit by molten gold, skidding out, and then crashing.

He looked at Goldar and his teammates, then at the truck. He knew his father was inside and needed his help. *No choice*, he thought. The other Rangers could fend for themselves.

Jason launched out of his Zord and into a sea of putties. None of them stood a chance as he fought his way to his father.

Sam looked up and saw only the Red Ranger, not his son.

"Give me your hand!" Jason called out.

His father hesitated, unsure of everything happening around him.

"Look at me!" Jason continued. "Trust me! It's okay. You're all right."

His father reached out his hand, and Jason pulled him to safety.

Zack and Billy approached Goldar. For a moment they all paused . . . then Goldar slashed at them and knocked both Zords tumbling. "Jason, help us!" Billy yelled.

Jason pulled himself back into his Zord and rushed to their aid. "I'll take Goldar from the left!"

Trini's voice called out. "Jason! I'm right behind you!"

Overhead, Kimberly swooped down and picked up the triceratops as Billy curled it into a tight ball. Kimberly flew up thousands of feet in a few seconds . . . then circled around and dove.

"Incoming!" she shouted, and let the triceratops go.

CHAPTER THIRTY

Billy's Zord landed in front of Goldar with the impact of a huge bomb. Parked cars and newspaper boxes went flying. So did Rita Repulsa. She was catapulted over several buildings and landed in a heap. All of her putties collapsed into junk. Even Goldar was staggering, going down on one knee.

The Rangers cheered. "Billy, are you okay?" Zack yelled. "That was crazy brave, dude."

The triceratops rolled over and got to its feet. "I'm okay," Billy said, but he sounded a little spacey.

They all looked around. Had they won? Where was Rita?

They found out soon enough. Goldar formed a

hand beneath Rita and gently lifted her until she stood upright. The molten gold healed some of her wounds and as he swung her back around, her eyes locked in on the shattered ground around the Krispy Kreme. "I feel the Crystal," she said.

Goldar demolished the building to dig into the earth below the foundation. Before the Rangers could stop him, a blinding beam of light shot up from the hole. Goldar stopped and took a few steps back, admiring it.

The Rangers were transfixed for a moment. They had never seen anything so bright and pure. Then Jason got moving again. "He found the Crystal!"

One by one, the Rangers locked their Zords into a line between Goldar and the Zeo Crystal's hole. Goldar smashed into the line, driving forward. The road buckled beneath them. "We're sliding," Billy said. There wasn't much space between them and the blazing crater.

Trini chimed in. "It's getting hot in here."

Goldar shoved the line of Zords toward the Zeo Crystal's light. "Yes!" Rita exulted. "Push them into the hole! Let them melt!"

Inside the Zords' cockpits, the Rangers were starting to suffer from the heat. "This is it, guys," Jason said. The T. rex's armor was starting to buckle.

Trini saw that the mastodon was starting to warp out of shape. Zack had passed out from the heat. She sprang up to slap the mastodon's cockpit. "Zack!" Trini cried out.

He snapped awake. "I'm here!"

The Zords' armor groaned from the heat. They were at the edge of the hole. In another moment, they would topple in.

"Are we going over?" Billy screamed.

"No!" Kimberly thought she understood what might be happening. "Hold on tight to one another!"

The Rangers made one last push back against Goldar's irresistible force. Crushed between Goldar's heat and the energy of the Zeo Crystal, the Zords began to fuse together. The mastodon connected to the T. rex, the saber-toothed tiger to the triceratops and the pterodactyl. All around them was the Zeo Crystal's brilliance—but it wasn't destroying them. It was . . .

They stood up together from the edge of the burning

crater. "Guys!" Billy called out. "We're like one big Zord. Like a mama Zord. No, that sounds lame. A Megazord!"

They had become a single Megazord as big as Goldar, with a glowing opening in its chest that blazed with the energy of the Morphin Grid. All five Rangers were part of it, and from their cockpits they each controlled different parts of its body. From the edge of destruction, they had bonded together to find their ultimate strength.

Outside the Krispy Kreme, Rita Repulsa stood astonished by the sight of the Megazord rearing up out of the burning pit. "How?" she wondered. Few Power Ranger teams could form a Megazord even after years together. But these . . . children! . . . had managed it after barely an hour.

She stepped up onto Goldar's hand and melded herself into his torso. It was time to teach these children a lesson before they learned how to pilot the Megazord.

CHAPTER THIRTY-ONE

"Everyone, let's go!" Jason called out.

The Megazord staggered as the Rangers tried to control it. It wobbled a bit before toppling over with an impact strong enough to shatter the windows in nearby buildings.

"I think that might have been my fault," said Billy. "I'm sorry."

"I think Kimberly needs to move our feet! Try again," Jason added.

"No. I've got an arm," Kimberly replied.

"I got a leg," Zack added.

"You're a leg, too?" Billy asked.

Trini chimed in. "I have the other arm."

"We all have to move together," Jason said. "All together on three. One . . . two . . . three . . ."

The Megazord slowly rose and pulled itself to its feet. This time, it kept its balance. They were getting the hang of it . . . just in time for Goldar to crash into them and drive them toward the docks.

"I can punch him!" Trini guided the Megazord's hand through a sweeping roundhouse. It made an awesome crash on Goldar's head. Goldar stumbled, crushing much of Angel Grove's waterfront boardwalk.

"Oh, that was so cool!" said Billy. "I wish I had an arm!" He activated his leg and knocked Goldar back.

The Rangers' early success was cut short as Goldar reeled back with his giant sword.

"Jason," called Zack, "you got anything for that?"

"Remember the Pit?" he asked.

"Yeah!" Zack replied.

The Megazord rushed Goldar, hitting him in the middle of his body. They ducked under his swing and lifted him up. Then came the final move: The Megazord body slammed Goldar to the ground.

The Rangers were starting to get it figured out. They threw another punch. The Megazord's fist crashed into the side of Goldar's face and knocked him flat.

"Stomp him!" Zack said, and they did, pounding on the golden monster until he started to go limp.

The Megazord picked up Goldar and shook him, flinging molten gold into the harbor.

"Kim, Trini!" Jason called out. "Move back the arms! We've got swords!"

With that, the Megazord unclipped the wings on its back that became two awesome swords.

"Wait!" Rita Repulsa's voice cut through the chaos as the Megazord plunged its sword through Goldar's chest, pinning him to the ground. The Megazord loomed over the defeated Goldar as Rita emerged from his chest onto his hand. Molten gold dripped and streamed from her. Goldar could barely hold her up. She looked up at him, sad that he was hurting. "Look at me." Rita turned to the Rangers. "You think you've won?"

The Power Rangers said nothing.

Rita pulled her coin from the head of her staff. "I came for the Crystal. Others will come! What you have? It can't last! You know I'm right!"

"I don't know," Jason said. Again, he wondered what the whole story was between her and Zordon. "But for now, I need you to give your staff and your coin to us. We will take you to Zordon and let him be the judge."

The mention of Zordon's name transformed Rita's expression to pure malice. "Zordon, judge me?" she said, her voice a hiss. "Never. No matter what Zordon says . . . I know I am worthy."

She thrust her staff toward the morphing energy that swirled in the Megazord's torso—but she was too slow. The Megazord reeled back a giant hand and, with all its power, batted her away. The force of the blow was enough to launch Rita into space.

"Did you just slap her?" Billy asked, not believing what had just happened.

"I did," Jason replied. "Weird, right?"

As she disappeared, Goldar sank to the ground. His form melted back into a thousand streams of molten gold that split into tinier and tinier rivulets. These sank into the ground and disappeared. In seconds, it was as if Goldar and Rita Repulsa had never existed.

The Rangers looked out over the town of Angel Grove. The brilliant shaft of light from the Zeo Crystal still shone up out of the ground. They had saved it. Maybe they had saved a lot more than that.

People emerged from hiding and began to surround the Megazord. The Rangers in their cockpits looked out at the people, who cheered and took photographs.

"I told you we'd be famous," Zack said as the Rangers celebrated.

Then Zordon's voice filled the air.

"Rangers," he said. "Hear me when I say, I am so proud of all of you."

Alpha 5's voice could be heard in the background. "Yeah, but you said they would fail!"

"Shut up, Alpha 5, I'm talking!"

Later, Jason entered Zordon's control room and walked straight to the chair. He set the sword back into its sheath.

"You should keep that," Zordon said from behind him. "You earned it."

"I'll come back for it," Jason said. At the door, he stopped to wave. Alpha 5 waved back. Jason had a feeling he would be seeing them again fairly soon.

EPILOGUE

Things slowly returned to normal in Angel Grove. Construction crews worked to rebuild the downtown. The Cascadia mine was gone. The Zeo Crystal had been hidden again.

Nobody in Angel Grove suspected that five high-school kids had saved the world . . . especially these kids.

Jason walked into detention. He smiled at Kimberly and then at Billy. He looked around and saw Trini, who smiled back. He took his seat as Zack strolled in. Zack gave the room a once-over before taking a seat behind them, next to an empty desk with a green jacket hanging on the chair.

The five Power Rangers all shared a sly smile as they pondered Zordon's words to them:

This Ranger team did what my team did not. You will humbly walk amongst your peers, but heroes you all will be. Each of your names will be etched alongside the great Ranger teams before you. I will always owe a debt of gratitude to you all.

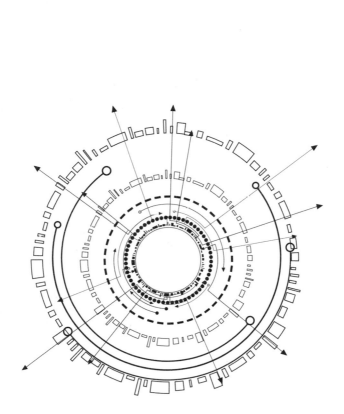